# Tybee Sunrise

## A NOVEL

Grace,
May you always be
surrounded by love
and family.
( Just to remind you,
you are one of my "favorite
favorite bosses and "teacher")
Jim Waller
2014

# JIM WALLER

PUBLISHED BY HIGH PITCHED HUM PUBLISHING
www.highpitchedhum.net

HIGH PITCHED HUM and the mosquito are trademarks of
High Pitched Hum Publishing.

ISBN: 978-0-9885818-7-6

*To Marjorie and all "Island Girls" no matter
the geography or terrain on which they nurture their own
visions of love and family*

Call it a clan, call it a network, call it a
tribe, call it a family: whatever you
call it, whoever you are, you need one.

—*Jane Howard, British novelist*

# One

$\mathcal{M}$att Ryan locked the door of his office and walked out onto Butler Avenue. After a short stroll, he turned left onto Tybrisa Street. It was a little after four, perhaps a bit early for a drink, but everyone knows that Alan Jackson and Jimmy Buffet long ago affirmed that it's always five o'clock somewhere. Besides, Tybee time could be anything he wanted it to be. He was eager to begin the search for Carolyn, but first he needed to get a feel of his new home. When he left her for Yvette ten years ago, Carolyn married a banker from Savannah and moved south. After the bitter divorce from Yvette, Matt brushed away the shadows concealing Carolyn in a suppressed corner of his heart and freed her to reclaim the place she had dominated through high school and into college.

Interloping into another man's romance was something he had never considered, but with Carolyn perhaps he would. And who knows? Many changes can occur in a decade. Was she still married? Was her husband still alive? His demise was not a possibility Matt would joyously embrace—but it would be convenient. And what about Carolyn? Would the pain of the way he had dumped her be forgiven by now? He didn't know, but he had to find her.

Walking toward the sea along Tybrisa, the smells of pizza and beer and ice cream greeted his nostrils. He reached a bar that someone had recommended and stepped inside. The cooler temperature suddenly swathed his body and he involuntarily shivered. He was surprised by that effort of his body to warm him. He was used to the cooler weather of the Northeast and liked it. Then he remembered the cooling effect of humidity on sudden temperature change. It was like coming out of the Atlantic back home on Long Island in May and facing a brisk northeast wind.

He seated himself at a table and ordered a beer. Half way through the drink, a boisterous young man challenged anyone in the house to a game of pool. Matt figured he had nothing better to do and agreed to take the kid on. After the first round—that Matt won—the boy suggested a small bet on another game. Matt accepted and won the break and a small sum of money.

The stakes were raised and the games continued. In a short while, Matt began losing. Almost an hour of play passed, and it dawned on Matt that he was being hustled. He laid the cue stick on the table and stood staring at the boy.

"What?" the hustler asked innocently.

"You know what. You just hustled me out of eighty dollars."

"No, man, I play the game. It was your choice. Nobody made you play."

Matt walked around the table to where the boy stood. The young man gripped his cue stick in a defensive mode. The bartender, the waitress, and the four tourists stopped in mid-animation and looked at the two men. Matt whispered so low that only the boy could hear, "I ought to kick your ass. But today is your lucky day. Mark it on your calendar." Matt returned to his table.

The noise level from the tourists in the street outside began to rise above the music in the bar. Matt finished the first drink and ordered another beer. Ordinarily he would have had wine, but in the Georgia heat and humidity here on Tybee Island he found beer more refreshing.

The waitress brought the second round. Evening customers had not yet begun filling the bar, so the waitress sat across from

Matt and started a conversation. She had already concluded he would be good for a generous tip, but why not sweeten the pot?

"Where you from, cowboy? I noted from your accent you aren't from around here."

Matt studied the girl's features for a moment. She was a little overly made-up, but definitely pretty in an earthy sort of way.

"Actually I'm not a cowboy at all, unless you want to consider the occasional rides on my ex-wife's horses that sometimes made me feel like a 'cow puncher,' as John Wayne would say. I'm a lawyer from New York City. I just opened a new office here on the island. You need any legal services?"

"Not at the present. But if I do, I definitely will let you know." She paused for a moment then added, "Especially now that you mentioned an ex-wife. Let me tell you about my ex. Now there's a story you want to hear."

The waitress began the story of her ex's dalliances with some of the local gentry while she was working, and how he had insisted on alimony after the divorce.

Between waiting on customers that had begun straggling into the bar, she returned to Matt's table to continue the story—and perhaps cultivate a new romance. On the last return to Matt's table, she pointed to a middle-aged man with a young woman seated beside him hanging on his every word and frequently laughing, apparently at his jokes.

"See the guy there with that gorgeous lady? He's a Savannah lawyer. You want me to introduce you?"

Before Matt could protest, the waitress was at the other table pointing in his direction. The man looked at Matt and motioned him to join them. Matt would not be rude. The man stood and extended his hand as Matt approached the table.

"I'm Bruce Bradley." He pointed to the woman still seated. "This is my wife Corrine. Isn't she a knockout? She's a nurse."

Matt introduced himself and went through the usual greetings and getting-to-know-you ceremonies. After a time of everyone becoming comfortable with each other, Bruce mentioned that since Matt was new in town and single, it was time for him to get acquainted with some of the local ladies.

"I'm not presently in the market," Matt quickly answered. "I sort of have someone."

"One more won't hurt," Bruce declared and laughed. "You can never have too many of them—if you know what I mean." He winked at Matt and laughed again. Corinne looked down at the top of the table, her expression unchanged. Bruce glanced at her and frowned. "I'm going to make a phone call. I know a beautiful young lady, one of Corinne's nurse friends, who would be perfect for you."

Matt looked at him and wondered how he had made that assessment in the short time they had known each other. Despite Bruce's grooming, good looks, and profession, Matt thought he looked a little seedy. He definitely sounded like a jerk.

"You might as well get to know at least one nurse. There's one or two behind every oleander bush around here. But that's a good thing. If you need medical care, there's plenty available in Chatham County."

In less than a half hour, Bruce announced the nurse's arrival. Matt turned to look at her as she walked through the door and made her way through the gathering crowd. She was dressed in pink pants, a matching top, and white deck shoes. Matt's first impression of her was that she was short and could be considered by some a little plump around the middle, not at all tall and dark like Carolyn. He concluded immediately that this nurse was not his type.

He started to turn away, but her confident and striking gate drew his focus. He scanned her body and noted that her breasts looked firm and in perfect symmetry with her hips. For a reason he could not explain, his indifference began to subside. His gaze eased upward to her face drawing him like a magnet. Her honey-colored skin was smooth as a porcelain doll. Her subtly colored lips were full and looked soft as warm butter. Her nose was perfectly shaped and blemish free. Her wide, sloe-shaped eyes were the color of a cloudless summer sky. Hair matching the color of her complexion curled outward at the ends slightly below her shoulders. Matt stared hypnotically. He wanted to turn away but could not.

Her walk to the group's table was extraordinarily feminine. Her gait was leisurely and effortless without conscious effort to make it so. The placement of each of her small feet seemed to fall into the plane of the previous step. She greeted the group with a soft smile. Bruce stood up and hugged her tightly to his breast and kissed her on the cheek near the dimple at the corner of her mouth. For a moment Matt felt a twinge of jealousy. He felt he should have been the one to greet her in that manner. *What is wrong with me? I don't even know this woman. Besides, didn't I come here to find Carolyn?*

"Matt, I want you to meet Melody Malone, one of the finest nurses in the county, and if for some foolish reason you don't run away with her, I will." Bruce looked at Corinne, obviously not pleased with that declaration and her husband's "friendly" manner with another woman.

Melody tried to hide the embarrassment and pain she felt for Corinne. She smiled and nodded subtly. Except for Matt, everyone's attention turned to Bruce, who kept up constant chatter and off-color jokes. Melody smiled softly and attempted to steer the conversation in a different direction. Matt could turn his attention away from her for only brief moments. His mind returned to the reality of his yearning for Carolyn from time to time, and he wondered what was happening to him. He came south hoping to find a lost love, not a new one.

After half finishing a margarita, Melody announced that she hated to leave good company, but she had to go.

"I'm ready to call it a night, too. I'll walk out with you." Matt said his goodnights without acknowledging Bruce's suggestion that they should get together again soon. Matt instinctively disliked Bruce. He was the kind of lawyer that gave the others a bad name.

He and Melody stepped onto sultry, unquiet Tybrisa Street busy with tourists of every variety. The couple walked past young—and not so young—tourists in bikinis, and a woman wearing a thong barely covering her nether regions. Two young men across the street stared at her and weaved unsteadily as they sipped from plastic cups. One of the men gave a muddled wolf whistle and one of his sandaled feet slipped from the curb. His friend caught him before he fell to the ground and both struggled to regain their footing. The woman ignored them and kept walking. A light breeze wafted from the ocean. The full moon almost directly overhead cast an enchanting glow on Melody's face.

"Can I walk you home?" Matt asked.

"It's such a beautiful night out, do you mind if we stroll around a bit?" Melody looked up into Matt's face. He was already looking at hers.

"No, I don't mind at all. I would love that."

The couple walked slowly to the pavilion and onto the pier. In a darkened place, Melody stopped and leaned on the rail looking into the surf falling gently on the shore. Matt followed and stood close to her, their arms touching. They scanned the moon glade sparkling on the water like strobe lights on a trail of white diamonds. They stood silent for a minute or two watching the ebb and flow of the tide. After a while Melody spoke, her voice floating soft and smooth like a mellow love song.

"I'm glad you left the bar with me. I would have been heartbroken if you hadn't."

"But you ignored me all evening."

"You're a stranger, and I'm a lady."

Matt looked down at her and smiled. "And you ladies do have your ways. You should have let me know something, given me a clue. You didn't even look at me all evening. What if I had let you leave alone?"

"I knew you were watching me. I left early because I knew you would leave with me."

"You knew that?" Matt straightened from leaning on the railing. "I don't believe this!" he said with mock disbelief. "And you would take a chance that you could miss an opportunity to meet a great guy—meaning me, of course." They laughed.

"Would you care to walk down the beach a ways?"

"Sure. We can do that."

Melody walked away and Matt followed her. They descended the steps from the pier onto the beach.

"I can't navigate this sand in these shoes," Matt protested.

"Of course you can't. Take them off." Melody removed her shoes and began rolling the bottoms of her pants. "Roll yours as high as you can," she ordered. Holding her shoes in one hand and Matt's hand in the other, she led him to the water's edge. They walked along the shoreline toward Back River, the body of water separating Tybee from Little Tybee. Near the estuary of the river, they stopped and stood looking out over the moon-lit water. They stood a long while silently breathing in the beauty before them. Melody took a deep breath as if summoning courage and moved closer to Matt and took both of his hands in hers. He turned from the ocean and looked into her face. She raised her head and their gaze met in the glow of the moonlight. He moved his arm around her waist and drew her to him. Her warm body melted into his. He should stop now before it was too late and take this woman home. He breathed the fragrance of her hair and thought of lilac. Intoxication swept over him and he knew he was approaching the point of no return. He kissed her, gently at first and then urgently. A series of soft moans rose up from somewhere deep inside her.

After a long time that seemed a mere instant, Matt raised his head and looked over melody's shoulder. Fifty feet or so behind her, a small grove of palm trees stood near the trough of two high sand dunes. He took her hand and steered her in that direction. She made no effort to stop him.

She knew immediately where they were headed and thought she should protest, but she could not. A wanting stirred inside her, urgency she had never before felt with a man, and certainly not with someone she had just met. Was there really such a thing as love at first sight?

Men came on to her frequently, but she was rarely moved by their approach. Young Dr. Morehouse had been pestering her since he came to the pediatrics wing of the hospital last spring. He was nice and she liked him and he had her attention. But she was not sure she was ready to give in to his advances.

She had not been with a man for more than a year. She had her work and the activities of the island, and she was happy. Now, here she was with this stranger awakening feelings in her that she had neither sought nor expected. But there they were, loosed and unrestrained, saturating every pore of her body. Humidity seemed to rise and caress her, and the night suddenly felt hot. The stranger in her arms would be gone in the morning never to be heard from again. She would hate herself, and Regret would take his place as her new companion. But for now all resistance had flown from her, and she would fight no more—at least not tonight.

Matt's grip of her hand tightened, and she followed him toward the place where he was leading her for what she eagerly anticipated would happen. Brief thoughts of resistance gripped her, but she forced them from her mind before she could act. She should turn now and run home as fast as she could. The guilt that she knew would be hers in the morning was already nagging at her. She had been with a man or two, but she had never felt like this before, and she was afraid.

They reached the place where the New York stranger was leading her and she was glad.

# Two

$\mathcal{I}$ t was two days ago that Matt aimed his S-Class Mercedes-Benz south on I-95, and pushed it as hard as he thought he could get away with. It was not that he disliked New York City. He needed to outrun the pain he was feeling. The morning sun had skirted above the city skyline, and before nightfall he would be in Savannah and Tybee Island to begin a new life. The bitter divorce was final now, and Yvette and her new boy-toy would soon be far behind.

He had met Yvette shortly before they graduated from Harvard Law School. Following their graduation in 2002, Emile Bordeaux brought his daughter and her new husband into the firm that became Bordeaux, Ryan, and Ryan. Now it would be Bordeaux and Yvette's New Harvard Man-Slut. *Let's see if he can grow the firm as I did, helping to make it one of the most successful corporate law firms in the city.* A bitter smirk curled on Matt's lips.

He did not regret his contributions to the firm. He would leave it with a payout of three million dollars. With the extra million in guilty-conscience money from Yvette, and his four million in various investments, he would do OK in the friendlier cost-of-living in the South. The spacious condo overlooking the Atlantic Ocean on Tybee Island was already paid for and furnished at a remarkably reasonable price. No more snow; no more ice; no more hurry-hurry.

When he and Yvette visited the island four years ago, he was immediately infatuated with what the locals referred to as "Tybee time," a laid back approach to life without the encumbrance of clocks and absolute schedules. He looked forward now to the slower pace. He had always thought he would retire young on Long Island. But after discovering Tybee, his dream changed to settling there some day. That would not be easy. Yvette probably could not be dislodged from their home in the Hamptons.

But Yvette was not a problem now. He could go wherever he pleased and do whatever he wanted. His ambition in early life was to make a lot of money, and he had done that. When he married Yvette, he thought her money would guarantee happiness. For a while he was happy, and then he was not. Maybe it was not dollars that he needed after all.

He had rented a small office on the island and a sign had been put up. He would have someplace to report to and pick up some business to keep him in the loop, and keep the wealth he had accumulated in his pocket.

Driving south now on I-95, Matt thought of Yvette's deception and winced at the pain invading his heart in bitter waves. He had struggled to move beyond her money and prestige and fall in love with her, and he had finally succeeded. His demanding work schedule had blinded him to her growing aloofness over the last several months of their marriage. And even though he missed the attentiveness of the past, infidelity was the last thing he would suspect.

Damn that early agreement on the Fishburne case! Another hour of negotiation and he would have gone straight home. But he didn't. He went by his office to pick up the briefs on the McIntyre hearing scheduled for the next morning. And there she was, sprawled out on the carpet with that boy looking half her age going at her like a sex-addicted rabbit on Viagra, her panties wrapped around one leg, his underwear tangled around his ankles. And to add insult to injury, it was Matt's brand new carpet laid the day before. He said nothing, but Yvette turned her head and looked at him. Engrossed in the business at hand, the boy atop her did not notice Matt or miss a stroke. Matt's sharp, analytical mind morphed into a functionless blob, and he neither moved nor thought. When he finally gathered himself, he turned and walked away.

He didn't know how he got there, but his next awareness was of lying on his bed facing the wall with his knees hugged tightly to his chest. Rejection by a woman he had grown to love crashed upon him in convulsive waves. He lay trembling through the night. Occasionally his eyes moistened and overflowed onto the pillow. He had to do something, but he did not know what.

Again, he was betrayed by someone who was supposed to love him and be with him through good times and bad. Finally he fell into a fitful sleep. And when he awoke in the morning, he was still lying in the same position he remembered from the night before. He looked around and listened. He saw nothing and heard nothing. Apparently Yvette had not come home last night.

The trembling of his body was gone now, and he stretched out on his back and stared at the ceiling all day. When he felt that night had fallen, he found his phone and called a friend that specialized in family law.

He dragged himself to the kitchen and lifted a frozen pizza from the refrigerator. He placed it in the microwave and set the timer. He stood staring at the wall, and the microwave began to beep. Several minutes passed, and when awareness finally awoke him to the reminder beep, he retrieved the pizza and slowly sliced it into four small pieces. He picked up a slice and took a bite. Staring blankly at the wall, he chewed slowly for a long time and finally swallowed. He laid the slice of pizza on the plate beside the other three. He stared without seeing the food before him.

Three or four minutes passed with a painful memory squeezing the temples of his head. Awareness of the pizza finally wedged its way into the pain, and he smiled sardonically remembering the pizza served for the free breakfast at his elementary school. He hated those free meals. The teachers tried to be discreet, but the children in his classes were not stupid. They knew. He picked up the plate and emptied the pizza into the garbage receptacle and stumbled back to bed.

Driving much faster than he should now on I-95 South, Matt could not purge from his mind memories of Yvette's infidelity and the night of the incident. He almost smiled at the irony of his wife getting laid by a new boy on his newly-laid carpet. *What the hell*, he thought and let the smile go ahead and happen.

Time, miles, and the Hardeeville, South Carolina exit ramp passed. He pressed harder on the accelerator, and in a short while sailed across the Savannah River and zipped through Pooler, Georgia. He knew his destination was near. He glanced at his phone. Thirty-one miles and he would be home on Tybee Island. The next exit would be I-16 East toward downtown Savannah. He slowed to make the turn. *What the hell*, he thought and punched the accelerator harder. Nearing the city he glanced to his left at the Eugene Talmadge Bridge hovering majestically above the big river. He checked his Breitling Chronomat. The trip had taken less time than he and his phone had calculated.

He decided to take a quick drive down River Street. He smiled at the thought. It would have to be a very slow drive. Speed on those ancient ballast stones would shake every bolt and screw off the Mercedes like berries from a lightening-struck bay tree. He took MLK Boulevard straight onto River Street and jostled along the ballast stones past the Hyatt Regency Hotel. He drove slowly, partly to preserve the integrity of the car, partly to observe the shops, restaurants, and bars along the ancient roadway, and partly to relive in his mind his first visit four years ago. He rolled down the windows to smell again the aromas of the street: food to suit every taste, beer, candy, and pastries. He inhaled a deep breath of cool salt air wafting up the river from the Atlantic nineteen miles east. He made his way slowly past places with colorful names: *309 West River Street, where the girls dance on the bar, Wet Willie's, True Grits, Fabulous Finds (under $20), Savannah Sweets, Jezebel, and One Eyed Lizzie's.*

Suddenly he gasped a quick breath and slowed almost to a stop when he saw a young woman walking along the sidewalk.

Was that Carolyn? He couldn't be so lucky. She had occupied a huge place in his mind even after he had dumped her for Yvette. After the divorce from Yvette, he found himself obsessed with the need to look for Carolyn, even though he had no clue as to what her response to seeing him again would be.

The woman on the sidewalk was slim and modestly proportioned. Her long, straight, black hair hung below her shoulders. He braked the Mercedes to a stop to get a better look. Could that really be her? The woman turned and smiled at Matt, but she was not Carolyn, his first and only sweetheart before Yvette. Disappointed, he drove on with thoughts of Carolyn lingering in his mind. He wondered what his life would have been like had he married her as he had planned and promised. In high school they talked often of their life together after they were married. Their relationship was close, comfortable, and warm, but their most intimate experiences had been French kissing and fondling. That changed in college when they learned about contraceptives and Carolyn's ease at obtaining prescriptions.

Memories of Carolyn now washed away every other thought as the onslaught of remembering her swept into his mind like a Savannah summer downpour. She was gorgeous in every way a woman could be gorgeous. In the photo in Matt's mind, a broad smile covered Carolyn's classical Latin facial features like those of her first-generation Italian-American mother. Even when he awoke with Carolyn in early morning, her face glowed as if lavished with olive-colored moisturizer. Her personality was usually business-like and serious. As she and Matt matured, she would sometimes go off on him unexpectedly, but the good times were worth the occasional firestorm. She was a brilliant student. In their early days of law school, she was there to help him through some of his most difficult exams.

Thinking of her now, he felt a subtle stirring in his groin. He remembered legs that he used to think as going all the way from the floor to an ass so tight she couldn't pass a banana seed, and a chest so narrow he could fondle both breasts simultaneously with one hand. Making love with her was the warmest, most pleasant experience a young man could imagine. On the coldest Massachusetts mornings when snowfall would thankfully steal away electricity and heat, her body would melt into his like tropical surf as they made use of the time classes were delayed or canceled.

Yvette could offer him financial stability, and he wanted that, needed that. His mother never held a job outside the home, and his father eked out the barest existence from his job in the vineyards near Buffalo where Matt grew up.

Those were the "good" times before the accident. He was eight then. Following his parents' burial, Matt felt abandoned and wondered how God could do that to him. Against her husband's wishes, Matt's aunt took him in. She loved him and he could see some of his mother in her, but the aunt offered affection and other support in secret only. Her husband did not like Matt and begrudged the pitiable dollars his wife spent on the boy. He avoided his uncle as much as possible. After his parents' death, and despite his aunt's love, he never again felt wanted or a part of a family.

From age ten he worked, first as a newspaper carrier, then in the vineyards and other jobs, some as disgusting and dirty as cleaning rabbit cages for a commercial breeder. Even now decades later, the thought of that job and the smell of ammonia and urine would overwhelm his nostrils and send him scurrying to a private place to avoid the possibility of an embarrassing response.

Always he saved most of his money. At an early age, he vowed to find a way to never again wear "no name" shoes from discount stores. He would be a lawyer and attend Harvard and wear Nikes and New Balance, and never again have to accept free lunches.

In high school he worked at a local grocery store, played outstanding shortstop on the school baseball team, and excelled academically. With merit and athletic scholarships following graduation, along with the money he had saved, he made it to the university of his dreams, but he still had to work to stay the full course. When he met Yvette, the money and prestige of an internship with her father's firm looked a lot better than minimum wage manning the serving lines in the university cafeteria.

Jostling now along the ballast stones on River Street in Savannah and thinking of the past, he thought of the Faustian character. Had he like Faust sold his soul? Had he given up the woman he loved then and even now could not get out of his mind?

He loved his job in New York, and over time he fell in love with Yvette. He was grateful for the opportunity she had given him to rub elbows with the elite of the city, and the power he commanded. As time went by, life with her and with his profession became as comfortable as three-year-old underwear. Life as he knew it would go on forever, or for as long as he wanted it to. Then he would retire on Long Island and live the life of a moneyed gentleman.

Unlike some of his colleagues, he had never cheated on his wife. He made vows and he would keep them. But Carolyn remained a warm memory and a love that he could not shake.

Two years after his marriage to Yvette, he ran into Carolyn at a seminar. And even though her attitude toward him was cool and aloof, they spent the day together. Over lunch she spoke of her plans to marry J. Randolph Winston, a middle-aged banker from Savannah. Matt attempted to dissuade her from going down south. He was married now and could not have her, but an empty feeling tugged at his heart thinking of her being so far away.

"What makes you think you will like the South with those strange-talking people, and the bugs and humidity, and people with double names or initials for names?" Remembering all of that now, Matt knew that Carolyn was a big part of the allure that brought him to the area. He wished to do nothing to harm her or interfere with her marriage. She was probably unavailable to him now—even if she could forgive him.

But sometimes people, places, and selfish thoughts creep into even the most innocent, unaware, and uninviting mind.

# Three

$\mathcal{D}$riving south on River Street, Matt remembered the Waving Girl statue near the Marriot Hotel and slowed the Mercedes to take a look. The ballast-stone roadway had been replaced by asphalt here and was smooth and easy riding. He pressed the accelerator a little harder. At Bay Street he hung a right and then a quick left onto Broad. He continued on Broad Street past the Pirates House Restaurant to the overhead sign marking President Street and Islands Expressway. At the traffic light, he swung a left. He steered the car past General McIntosh Boulevard and the railroad tracks and coasted to a slower speed. He saw no need to hurry now. Tybee time was just a few small islands away.

Approaching Harry Truman Parkway, he glanced to his right at a movement of some kind. In a fraction of a second, he realized the brief vision was of a man. He drove slowly onward with the disquieting vision roiling in his mind. His lawyer curiosity overtook his better judgment, and at the first opportunity, he turned the Mercedes around and drove slowly back toward the overpass. Before reaching it, he steered to the shoulder and turned off the engine. He stepped from the car and walked cautiously toward the spot where he had seen the movement. He approached slowly unknowing what he would find. The man could be an escaped convict or a serial killer, or

Lord knows what. A voice from the opposite end of the concrete truss supporting the overpass startled Matt.

"What is it you're looking for, mister? Whatever it is, it left on the last train to Albuquerque." The man spoke with a strong, clear, voice.

"I beg your pardon," Matt said after a long moment to gather himself.

"What is it you want here? If you are one of those do-gooders trying to take me to the mission, forget it. I'm happy right here. I can go to the mission anytime I want to."

*What the hell am I getting myself into?* "I was curious and stopped to help. Is there anything I can do for you?"

"What makes you think you can do something for me? Is it because you are driving that Mercedes there and wearing that Holland & Sherry suit and those Bacco Bucci shoes? You may think I don't know about such things. But for your information, mister, I haven't always lived under this bridge."

"I just thought maybe—."

"Well don't think. There's nothing I need from you or anyone. Now you get in that fine automobile of yours and drive on down the road. If you will do that for me, I promise I won't come snooping around your home."

"This is really where you live?"

"You ask too many questions, mister. You might ought to move on."

At that moment, a large man looking like a Michael Clarke Duncan clone appeared from nowhere.

"Is this dude bothering you, John? If he is let me know and I'll take care of it for you." A stern look of concern covered the man's dark face. Matt thought again of what he may be getting himself into, something that all the lawyers in the country could not get him out of.

"No, I'm OK, Robert. This Fancy Dan here has nothing better to do than pester folks minding their own business on a hot June day." The man squinted in the sunlight and spoke with a slow mid-western drawl.

"You all are homeless?" Matt asked.

"What do you mean, 'you all?' You are in the South. At least you could have the courtesy to learn the language. The word is 'y'all.' And yes, we live here, but we aren't homeless. This is our home." The man stepped from the spot where he was partially concealed by the concrete buttress. He walked out—strolled—into an area where the weeds and grass had been trampled leaving a small clearing.

The man was tall with a stubble of gray-peppered beard. His graying hair was long and neatly unruly. Looking at it, Matt did not think "hippy" or "shaggy." The thought was "natural." The man's clothes were clean but un-pressed as if washed and dried in coin machines. His piercing, gray-blue eyes reflected a subtle look of sadness as if he had known tragedy, but was determined to make peace with the world as he knew it. The intense focus of his eyes seemed to see something beyond the ordinary, something beyond the commonplace. Except for the veiled look of sadness in his eyes, he looked nothing like the derelicts Matt had seen on the streets and in the alleys of New York City.

"Since you're so nosy and aren't going to leave us alone until you know it all, maybe you should tell us who you are." The man paused, obviously irritated by the stranger's imposition into his home. "You've got to be one of those do-gooder social workers—or a nosy lawyer, and that's even worse."

"I'm sorry you feel that way, but yes, I am a lawyer."

"And let me guess, from Philadelphia?"

"Now you're the one being nosy, and your smart-assed guess is way off base. Sorry to disappoint your cliché-clouded mind, but I'm not a Philadelphia lawyer. I'm from New York City."

"I'm sorry—in both cases: you're a lawyer, and you're from New York City."

"Well get over it, beggar-man—in both cases."

"Oh, we're into name-calling now—barrister."

Matt looked beyond the weeds and underbrush beneath the bridge, and the banter was over for now. He was more interested in what he saw. Dozens of men and women engaged in small talk sat on buckets, apple crates, and what seemed to be throw-away items of various sizes, shapes and colors. Some lay sleeping on strips of cardboard. But what demanded his attention most was an area nearest the expressway furnished like a normal living room—except there was no living room. A red lounge chair sat facing the river. Beside it a small end table, somewhat weathered looking, held a radio and a newspaper. Stacked on one corner of the table were books by or about Nietzsche, Kant, Descartes, Plato, and Bertrand Russell. A color-perfect sofa looking slept on faced the lounge chair. A small battery-powered TV lay screen down on a loveseat.

Winds from the southeast suddenly pirouetted from the northwest ferrying the faint smell of tobacco and cannabis to Matt's nostrils. Astonished at the unfolding scene, he could say nothing for several long seconds. He finally gathered himself and spoke.

"So this is your home?"

"Yes, it is."

"How do you secure and protect all of your belongings here?" Matt made an abbreviated sweep of his hand toward the "living room."

"I have a special security system." The man placed his hand on the clone's shoulder. "Would you steal anything from my friend here?"

Matt ignored the question. After a moment of silence, he folded his arms across his chest and said, "I apologize for calling you homeless."

"Then I apologize for apologizing for your home state and profession."

"Maybe we can now begin to be civil." Matt recognized in the stranger a compelling uniqueness, drawing him irresistibly to him like a finely-crafted classic novel liberally endowed with incomprehensible, obscure imagery and symbolism. He could not turn away. The man was not at all what Matt would expect a homeless person to be.

"I have to admit your place looks relatively comfortable, but how do you deal with the weather and bugs and the looks of pity from people you meet on the street?"

"Lately, barrister, my most common response to the slings and arrows life may throw at me is I don't give a rat's ass— which, in and of itself, is a rather ridiculous statement. I don't know anyone who would offer the posterior of a rodent. More than that, I don't know anyone who would joyously receive the gift."

"Homeless-man, you sound like one of those weird philosophers who use a thousand dollars worth of words to make a ten-cent statement."

"Bingo, barrister. I don't think of myself at all as weird, but I am a philosopher. You're smarter than I gave you credit for."

Matt stared at the man. Could he be serious? Could he possibly be an actual, certified philosopher?

"I see the doubt in your eyes, barrister. PhD from a midwestern university that I refuse to name. They wouldn't be proud of me now. I taught philosophy there until my wife turned me out and I came to Savannah."

"You're serious?"

"As a hurricane."

"So, you're a philosopher with a doctorate degree living under a bridge in Savannah, Georgia?"

"You find that hard to believe, barrister?"

"I find it totally incredible."

"Believe it, barrister. Thinking adults have a choice, and this is what I choose"

"Why don't we exchange names, so we can dispense with the left-handed character assassinations." Matt suddenly realized he was getting in too deep with a mental case or an addict or a fugitive from the law. Homeless-man had to be one or the other.

"My name is Matthew. I go by 'Matt.'"

"You can call me John, if you need to address me at all— which I find totally unnecessary."

Matt ignored the put-off. "Do you have a last name?"

"Wayne, if you just have to know."

"John Wayne. Your name is John Wayne?"

"That's right, barrister."

Matt had all he could tolerate from an ingrate he was

reaching out to. "Yeah, hell, you're John Wayne, your friend there is Robert Redford, and I'm Matthew McConaughey." Matt waved a hand in disgust and walked quickly toward his Mercedes. His mission was to find Carolyn, not waste time on riff-raff.

"Claim it, barrister. You look enough like the actor to be his brother—or at least a first cousin." He watched Matt hastily retreating and yelled after him, "But he can't possibly be as nosy as you are."

Matt ignored the statement and the loud laughter coming from homeless-man and the clone and did not look back. He threw himself into the car and started the engine.

Driving toward Tybee along Islands Expressway, thoughts of a strange man calling himself "John Wayne" and a philosopher lingered like a toothache that wouldn't go away. If the man was living the delusion of a philosopher, why didn't he call himself Friedrich or Immanuel or Rene` or Plato or Bertrand? *Damn. Why did I let myself get involved with that rude, irascible old coot? I'll make it a point to never see that s-o-b again.*

# Four

$\mathcal{M}$att drove to the end of Islands Expressway and merged onto U.S. 80. The sun behind him had by now melted into a half-inflated orange basketball. He crossed the Bull River Bridge and continued east on Tybee Road—US 80—past Fort Pulaski. The tide was unusually high, spilling over the banks of the south channel of the Savannah River, flooding the short land area up to the shoulder, but not over the highway. Except for a thousand islands of lush green marsh grasses, rippling white water covered the massive flood plain stretching into the horizon on the right side of the highway. Gentle waves broke softly on the shoulder of the roadway. A feeling of peace and calmness settled over him, and he no longer needed to hurry. The osmosis of Tybee time was already seeping into his soul like the humidity saturating his skin. He drove slowly on and smiled as he passed the parked police cruiser partially concealed behind huge oleander bushes near the boat-launch dock.

A few yards more, he topped the Lazaretto Creek bridge and was greeted by the beacon from the Tybee Island lighthouse. He drove on down First Street to the big curve at Butler Avenue. At Tybrisa Street he lined up behind vehicles negotiating a left turn. Dozens of tourists on the sidewalks and in the roadway meandered about as if strolling the meadows and woodlands of Central Park. He finally made the turn and fell behind other cars coasting slowly past the souvenir shops, art galleries, restaurants, lodgings, and bars.

He was almost home now. He reached his condominium, parked, grabbed a couple of pieces of luggage, and went inside. Night had fallen and the lights along the beach and roadways illuminated the tourists on the pavilion and pier, in and near the ocean and on the streets. He opened the patio door and listened to the sounds of waves breaking on the shore, and bands playing in the bars and eateries and on the pavilion. A festive atmosphere undulated on the sultry breeze. He thought he would go down for a drink and join the revelers, but he suddenly realized he was exceedingly tired. He left the door open and turned back to survey the room. He closed the door and walked to a bedroom and found the bed beckoning. He kicked off his shoes and fell upon the bed.

He slept soundly through the night and awoke later than he intended. The last thing he remembered was dreaming of Carolyn Parker. They were still at Harvard, and classes had been cancelled by a night-time blizzard, and they saw no reason to get out of bed. The dream lasted a long time, and he did not want to wake up.

He remembered the notation on the door of his office announcing operation hours of 10 a.m. to 5p.m. He bounded out of bed and rushed to the shower. To show up late for his first day would not make a complimentary impression. He turned on the water, but by the time it had warmed just right, the memory that he was now on Tybee time struck him. He smiled and relaxed. No one would be lined up at his door anyway. No one here knew him, and even if someone did notice that a new law office had opened, they probably wouldn't care. The real estate agent that sold him his condo had told him the most frequent, and about the worst, crime committed on the island was bicycle theft, and he didn't have one—yet. Everything on the island was accessible by foot or by bike, so he certainly intended to shop for one as soon as possible.

"And don't worry too much about your bicycle being stolen," the real estate agent had said. "The thief needs to get somewhere in a hurry, and when he gets to his destination, he'll lay it down and all you have to do is go get it."

Matt smiled at remembering that exchange. He dressed and without going by his office, went directly to a restaurant on Butler Avenue. He had coffee and a leisurely breakfast and read the June issue of the *Tybee Breeze*. He finally made it to his office around 11:30.

A woman in a motorized wheel chair sat outside his door anxiously looking up and down the street. He greeted the woman and inserted the key in the lock. She glared at him without speaking until they were inside.

"Where the hell have you been? Doesn't that damn sign on the door say 10 o'clock? I've been waiting here a hell of a lot longer than 10 o'clock. I'm going to make you a new hours-of-operation sign. It's going to say 'If the damn door is unlocked and the lights are on, I'm open; if the door is locked and the damn lights are off, I'm closed.' What if it was raining? Do you know how quick a summer shower can hit here?" The woman hesitated and slowly inhaled a labored breath.

Matt thought of answering no, he didn't know that, but he was struck speechless by the woman's language and behavior that belied her appearance of an aging Sunday-school teacher. She wore no makeup and her hair appeared to have had only a perfunctory brushing. The dress she wore was clean but plain. Her athletic shoes were scruffy and worn down on one side. White socks with elastic ribbing that had long ago vanished into oblivion fell around her ankles.

"Where in hell did you come from anyway?"

Matt was grateful that the attack had ended, and now the woman offered something he could respond to. "New York. I'm from New York City."

"Well hell fire and damnation. No wonder. You folks up there ain't got no friggin respect for no damn body. If you're going to make it here, sonny, you're going to have to learn some respect and manners."

Matt thought it interesting that even though the woman couldn't complete a sentence without a generous peppering of expletives, she had not used a single profane word.

"I'm sorry you're upset, and I'm sorry you feel the way you do about my home state. There seems to be an epidemic of that around here. Anyway, what can I do for you?" Matt could have responded differently, even ordered her from his office until she could be civil, but he couldn't help being amused. Behind her rough exterior he recognized softness and something likable about her.

"Aw hell, sonny, I didn't mean all that. I've never been to New York City. Never been north of South Carolina. All I know about the place is what I see in those friggin DeNiro and Pacino movies and, hell, I like them." The woman paused and her demeanor softened. "What's your name, sonny? I saw it on the damn door, but that was a thousand years ago while I was waiting for you. I've forgotten it by now."

"I'm Matt, I'm happy to meet you."

"That don't tell me much. You got a last name?"

"I do. Everybody has a last name, and so do I. I grew up poor, but we could at least afford a last name." Matt decided he would give the woman some of her own medicine and quickly added, "But we had only one, and the whole family had to share it. But all of us eventually got used to being called 'Ryan.'" Matt had begun liking her enough to tease her a little. Besides, why take things so seriously? This was Tybee Island.

"Oh, crap," the woman exclaimed. "Matt Ryan. Another damn Irishman, as if there's not enough of them around here already. Every time you stumble over a sand dune, a friggin Irishman jumps out."

"Well, I ought to feel right at home then, shouldn't I?" Matt would play her some more.

"Don't mock me, sonny. I may be in this damn wheel chair, but I can still swing this cane." She lifted the aged cane in her right hand and shook it at him.

"I'm sorry. I certainly wouldn't want the wrath of that fierce-looking cane."

"You're mocking me again, sonny."

---

"Yes ma'am, I am, and I will stop it. Tell me your name and what I can do to help you."

"I'm Florence Blalock from South Florida. I came here thirteen damn years ago."

"It's good to meet you, Florence."

"You will address me as 'Miss' Florence, young man. Do I have to keep reminding you that you're in the damn South now, and down here we adhere to certain social graces?"

"I apologize—Miss Florence. Now, what can I do for you?" An amused smile played on his lips.

"Well, it's my damn taxes. They're ninety-seven dollars more than they were last year. I sent them a damn check for the amount I paid then. They sent me this letter saying I have to pay the rest or file a friggin appeal. I called the county tax office and some prissy-assed girl—I know she was prissy-assed by her preppy talk. Anyway, this preppy-assed, sissy-girl said there were no exceptions. I had to pay or lose my friggin house." Miss Florence began to cough. A long spasm wrenched her entire upper body. Matt waited. The coughs finally subsided and she spoke again.

"Now I don't have the money, and I for damned sure ain't going to take this wheel chair all the way down highway 80 into town to argue a damned appeal. Matt—and it's socially acceptable in the South for me to call you Matt because I'm a hell of a lot older than you. Can you help me?"

Matt studied Miss Florence's demeanor for a moment before he answered. Why should he spend his own time and money for a charity he had no interest in? She was obviously suffering deep distress over the matter, but who would take valuable time to argue over a ninety-seven dollar tax bill? Ninety-seven million perhaps, but not a few measly dollars. Besides, what did he owe this rude old woman? Studying her countenance for a few seconds, he could see that this issue was as important to her as were the cases he defended for wealthy clients in New York. *What the hell. I have nothing better to do at the moment. I might as well help the old lady. Might help to scare up a paying client or two.*

"Miss Florence, I think I can help you. But tell me about your house. Real estate on the island is reasonable, but it doesn't come cheap. How did you come by your house if it stretches you that much to pay the taxes, which all-in-all seem fair to me."

"My mother's younger sister left it to me when she passed. I was living in a rented hovel at the time near every kind of jail bird and pervert you could imagine. And even though I was devastated by the death of my last living relative, I was grateful for the gift. It's a beautiful house. I want you to come around and visit sometime. I'll cook you a real Southern dinner every bit as good as Paula Deen's." She paused and thought for a moment. "Well, maybe not quite as good, but you will like it. Guaranteed," she added.

Matt noted the absence of expletives when Miss Florence spoke of her family.

"I'm going to help you with this problem, Miss Florence. Now you go on and enjoy your home."

Miss Florence rolled her wheel chair around Matt's desk and took both his hands in hers.

"Thank you, sonny. God bless you."

She turned the wheel chair toward the door. Before opening it she stopped and looked back at Matt.

"By the way, that damned Southern dinner is all the pay you're going to get. So you've got to be there at least one friggin time."

"Good bye, Miss Florence. But tell me, I've noticed with all your quite colorful language, you never actually curse. Is there a story in that?"

"Don't you question my religion, sonny. I'll have you know I'm a Christian, and I will not profane the name of the God that created me and set me down on this beautiful island." Miss Florence shook a pointed finger at Matt.

"I do apologize, Miss Florence. If you have any more problems I can help you with, let me know." She looked over her shoulder and smiled and waved to Matt. He watched her roll her wheelchair toward Inlet Avenue and disappear down 17th Street.

Matt decided he would go into town and see what he could do about Miss Florence's taxes. He locked the door to his office and noticed a young girl standing on the opposite corner watching him. She continued looking at him as he walked down Tybrisa to his condo. He looked at the girl and smiled. She continued looking at him and did not respond.

He got into his Mercedes and drove to Savannah. At the tax office, he inquired about a delinquent tax bill for a Miss— he made sure to use the title she demanded—Miss Florence Blaylock. He made the payment, and after a leisurely lunch on River Street—it seemed to him entirely appropriate that his lunch in Savannah be leisurely—drove back to Tybee.

The afternoon in his office passed with no more interaction, not even a phone call. A generous amount of time was spent day dreaming and fantasizing about Carolyn Parker. He wondered if she was still in the area. He knew she was married and wealthy now, and he was wasting his time thinking of her. But, heck, it didn't hurt to dream, especially since he had nothing else to do. He had to try to look her up as soon as possible, but things kept happening to keep him from his mission. And, he could not shake the trepidation he felt thinking of how she might react when he found her. If he could find her, maybe he would not even approach her; maybe he would simply look at her and remember.

# Five

$\mathcal{M}$att had been in the area two days now and still had made no move toward finding Carolyn. And even worse, here he was getting involved with another woman that he had met in a bar. He should turn away now, even though he knew he could not. She wanted this thing to happen. He knew that. And he wanted her. But he had another agenda that involved another woman. This would be a one-night stand and terribly unfair to the girl. He had never done this before, but what the hell. Her need for him made his urgency for her even more unstoppable, and desire for her had boiled far beyond his control. And even if he tried to walk away, he knew he could not. He had gone too far to turn back.

The couple reached the palm grove and sat in the trough of two high sand dunes. They kissed and Matt laid her gently onto the soft, warm sand. They continued kissing as Matt gently explored every inch of her body from her soft hair to the firm calves of her legs. Despite Melody's obvious eagerness for immediate contact, he began undressing her slowly and deliberately, feeling her anticipation rise in harmony with his own passion. He removed his shirt and lifted her onto it and continued to slowly undress her. He watched the moonlight caressing her body and began removing his own clothing. A brisk breeze rose out of the south, cooling them and blowing away whatever flying or hopping pests may be cruising the beach in search of dinner.

Matt constrained his passion and loved her for a long time. He would not hurry. After tonight Melody would be a memory. He would never see her again. Since he had gone this far and guilt would follow, he would take all that she offered.

Late into the night, the playful sounds of tourists in the surf and on the beach grew silent.

"Maybe we should get dressed and go," Matt said in the quiet. "It's getting kind of late. Nurses start work early, don't they."

"Yes, we do. But guess who's off tomorrow."

"Well," Matt started slowly, "you asked me to guess. Could it be Prince Charles? Nope. Couldn't be him. He's always off. Let's see, could it be Sean Hannity? No. He's always off, too."

"Come here, silly, and quit saying nasty things about people." Melody pulled him to her, and he felt the soft, moist warmth of her touch. He was happy that the guessing game was over.

Sometime later, Matt awoke to the whirring sound of a Coast Guard helicopter flying low overhead. He opened his eyes and closed them quickly against the morning sun glistening on the sand. By the time he could open his eyes again, the helicopter was making another low pass overhead. The pilot looked down at Matt and, with a wide grin, gave a thumbs up.

"Yeah, yeah," matt mumbled, throwing on his clothes quickly. "Semper Paratus, and all that."

He finished dressing and gathered clothing to cover Melody's body as she began to stir. The helicopter disappeared down the beach. Matt kissed Melody and stood up. He looked over the top of the ocean-side dune. With his left hand, he shielded his eyes from the glare of the sun rising over the pier. The sounds of voices wafted above the whisper of the surf at ebb tide. Over to his right toward Back River, a young couple frolicked along the edge of the water. He looked over his shoulder at Melody smiling and still lying with her eyes closed.

"You'd better get dressed, woman. The tourists are coming, and the Coast Guard may come back."

"The Coast Guard? What are you talking about?" Melody sat up and began dressing. "I'm talking about the Coast Guard helicopter crew that visited us a couple of times in our altogether."

"And you didn't cover me or anything?"

"I thought about covering you with me, but I didn't have the heart to deprive our heroes in arms."

"Oh, help me up!"

Matt laughed and pulled her to her feet. She turned away and covered herself as quickly as she could. She brushed sand from her clothes and hair, and tried to hide the embarrassment she felt in the morning light. Night nudity was one thing; daytime nudity another. Finally she joined Matt peering over the dune at a young couple running in and out of the surf.

Matt looked at Melody. Concern covered her face. "What do we do now? How do we get out of this mess?"

He did not answer immediately, but drew her to him and kissed her. After a long embrace, he held her at arm's length, staring into a face more mesmerizing in sunlight than it was in the glow of last night's moon.

"OK, here's our exit strategy," Matt announced finally. "Watch that couple down there, and when they run back to the water, we'll just tra-la-la out of here and amble on down the beach like Mr. and Mrs. Prim-and-Proper out for our morning stroll."

They followed the plan, and as they emerged from the dunes, they turned at the sound of soft footsteps on the dunes walkover to see an elderly couple holding hands, looking their way and grinning mischievously.

Matt walked with Melody to her apartment. He kissed her lightly at the door of her duplex and turned to leave. He looked across the yard, and on the deck of the large, beautiful house next door, Miss Florence watched from her wheelchair. Melody whispered, "She's a sweet old lady. Don't pay any attention to her. She's absolutely harmless." Matt, feeling a little sheepish, smiled and waved. Miss Florence returned the smile and wiggled an index finger from side-to-side in his direction.

"You've been a damn bad, boy," she said huskily with an exaggerated stern expression on her face. Matt walked on without responding.

After a quick shower and change of clothes at home, he stopped off at one of the famous restaurants on Butler Avenue. He finished breakfast and walked to his office. Before he unlocked the door he looked across the street. Standing on the corner looking at him was the young girl he had seen in that spot the day before. He paused for a moment feeling a little apprehensive. Was he being stalked?

Inside the office he sat for a long time thinking about Melody. She was a wonderful welcome to the island, but he would not see her again. He had to begin looking for Carolyn. He had promised to call Melody, but wasn't that what he was supposed to do?

No one came into his office, and the telephone sat silent. In the solitary quiet, the memory of last night's love making eased gently into mind. He had heard men say that in the dark, all naked women in your bed are the same. He had also heard it said that turned upside down all women look alike. His sexual experiences were limited, but as of last night, he knew those men were way wrong. Melody was different from the two other women he had known. The sensations her body offered were different, uniquely different, excitingly different. When he made love to her, they were no longer individuals mingling together. He felt himself totally immersed in her.

Sometimes, places or events or experiences in life strike so profoundly, so intensely that their impact on the psyche remains indelibly engraved forever. Thinking now of last night on the beach surrounded by Melody's love, he knew she was one of those experiences. Even if he followed his plan to never look into her face or speak to her again, she would always be a part of him.

Reminiscing alone now in the light of day, he almost smiled, but then he remembered his first impression of Melody: she was not his type. He sat for several minutes staring at the wall and wondering exactly what that meant, "not my type." Finding no reasonable answer, he decided to confront the philosopher with the question. That is, if he ever saw the rude old coot again, which he had no particular ambition to do. Besides, he needed to find Carolyn. He needed to know if she was available; and if so, would she forgive him for what he had done to their lives? And would he attempt a relationship with her if she were still married? Adultery was not something he would enthusiastically embrace. But to connect again with Carolyn, he would certainly consider it.

He wondered how much she had changed. Surely she had changed, at least some. Time always changes people. Money itself makes its own changes. He had seen that many times in the behavior of the nouveaux riche in sports, entertainment, and politics.

Surely she is a member of a local country club, a bridge club, and the League. Is she following a career, or is she simply a lady of leisure? And the big question is, can he find her? He wished he could remember her husband's name. Was it Wilson, or Williams? Seemed like something starting with a "W." Some Wilsons and Williams are wealthy, of course, but her husband's name sounded not only wealthy, but rich—really rich.

The ringing telephone startled Matt. Well, maybe some business. I hope this is a desperate caller needing desperate law advice and is willing and able to pay. Matt lifted the receiver and recognized the woman's voice.

"Hi. Called to see if you are up for a beer tonight. My treat. But I must warn you, I'm on the morning shift tomorrow, and as much as I enjoyed our night on the beach, I will have to sleep in my own bed tonight—alone and early."

"Oh, hey," Matt said, still not recovered from the start launched by the ringing telephone. Conflicting thoughts raced through his mind. A beer wouldn't hurt. But could he risk deeper involvement with Melody when his heart was set on reconnecting with Carolyn?"

"I, I would like that, but I really have something pressing that I have to take care of tonight." Matt immediately felt guilt at the lie. Melody sounded so innocent and trusting. But he had to protect his own interests, and at the moment she was not a priority, and he had no plans to make her one.

"Oh, OK. Maybe another time. Will you call me when it's convenient to get together?"

"Sure. I'll do that." Matt's guilt level escalated a degree or two, but he pushed it from his mind. *She's a nice kid, but hell, she's just not my type*. He thought of calling her back. Maybe that's what he should do. He recalled the sweetness, the innocence, the love he had found in Melody. Should he pursue a relationship with her or begin the search for Carolyn?

"I need to talk to somebody," he said aloud to himself. Then he remembered the "philosopher." Maybe he needed to see him sooner than he thought, even if the damn fool did think he is John Wayne and a real philosopher. He could be annoying for sure, but he also seemed wise. Maybe the old man could offer insight into the matter.

Matt locked the office and walked to his condo. He got into his car and drove the semi-circle around the Strand and 17th Street and turned west on Butler Avenue toward Savannah. He crossed Horsepen Creek, Lazaretto Creek, and Turner Creek. A short while later at Whitemarsh Island, he forked off US 80 onto Islands Expressway.

Nearing the Truman overpass, he steered the car onto the shoulder of the expressway and turned off the engine. He walked cautiously toward the place where he expected to find the philosopher. He felt no particular fear, but it wouldn't hurt to exercise caution. He looked down the row of "homes" beneath the overpass and into the first living room. The object of his visit sat in a lounge chair reading a book. The man looked up as the visitor approached.

"It's you again. Did you forget something here? Your wallet? Your obscenely expensive watch? Certainly not the keys to your Mercedes."

"I just want to talk to you, old man. Act civilized and I might even offer to take you to lunch."

"What makes you think I would go anywhere with you? Is it because little rich boy thinks he can flash his money around and everybody comes running?"

"OK, so you don't need a free lunch. What's wrong with a little civil company?"

"I have all the companionship I need right here." The philosopher gestured the length of the gatherings beneath the overpass. The clone, watching a talk show on TV, looked up and smiled.

"But I'll tell you what. I am hungry, and I'll let you spend some of your money." The philosopher laid the book aside and stood. He, the clone, and Matt walked to his car.

"Go up here to the traffic light and turn right. We're going down on River Street, then we're going to take a water taxi over to Hutchinson Island, and I'm going to let you buy me and Robert lunch at one of the most exclusive restaurants in the area."

"That's good. Whatever you say." In a moment of what Matt considered sanity, he wondered why he was even bothering himself with this old man thinking himself John Wayne and a philosopher.

At the restaurant they placed their order and sat for a moment looking at each other. Matt spoke.

"All right, old man, we've had our moment of mystery, now I want to know who you are—and I'm putting you under oath this time."

"Barrister, you aren't putting me under anything that I don't choose to be put under. I understand you feel free enough to order men like me around. Independent wealth makes you feel free, about as free as anyone can be in this life, and I know you are there. But I'm free, too. I don't possess anything, will never own anything, but I don't want to, and that's what makes me as free as you are."

The philosopher went silent but continued staring sternly at Matt who also remained silent, surprised by the philosopher's assertiveness. The clone squirmed in his seat. Matt turned away from the philosopher's glare.

"Now, I've already told you my name." The philosopher finally broke the uncomfortable silence. "I'm going to tell you one more time, that's it: John Marion Wayne. I never use the 'Marion' for the same reason **the** John Wayne didn't." The atmosphere had softened.

"And why was that?"

"Think about it, barrister. His birth name was Marion Robert Morrison. A name has a tremendous influence on the shaping of our lives. It sets the course of our lives forevermore. My parents were just like everyone else in my little hometown, ultra conservatives and lifelong John Wayne fans. They met at the theater where his movies were a regular fare. They loved his conservative, no-nonsense persona. They expected me to grow into a John Wayne clone. But at a certain point in my life I discovered Plato and other great philosophers.

"When I learned of Socrates' exhortation that a life unexamined is not worth living, I began to look at who and what I was. Over time I came to realize I was not what my parents and most of the people in my hometown were, nor would I ever be. As I matured I began to observe and think on a mature level and realize that things are not always what they seem. Some of the so-called 'important people' in my town led a day-time existence and a very dark night-time life. I left home for the university, and that sealed the deal for me. Among other revelations, I came to the conclusion that the difference between social conservatives and social liberals is that the first hide their behavior; social liberals don't give a damn. That changed my thinking a hundred and eighty degrees.

"But, back to names. What if Teddy Roosevelt's parents had called him Theodore or Ted? What if Chipper Jones' parents had insisted on calling him Larry? And then there's Lawrence Peter Berra. What if he had been addressed as anything other than Yogi? Think about it, barrister."

"So you really are John Wayne and a philosopher?"

"All the days of my life. And my friend here is really Robert."

"Well tell me, John Wayne, who other than lawyers and moneyed people do you hold in contempt?"

"Why do you ask that? I like wealthy people. I just don't need to be one. I am a committed egalitarian, and I don't believe greed is a complimentary human characteristic. That is not to say that all wealth is accumulated through greed. But look around you. The struggle to acquire things is rampant in the world. But this is nothing new. Thomas Wolfe addressed the issue in 1938. His take on greediness was 'I think the enemy is here before us with a thousand faces, but I think that all his faces wear one mask. I think the enemy is single selfishness and compulsive greed.' He wrote of greediness in his home town. That's one of the reasons he could not go home again.

"You mentioned lawyers. They are a necessary and valuable asset to a civilized society. And contrary to your misguided impression of me, there's a certain one that I love more than life itself."

"And who would that be?"

"You seem to have a nose problem, barrister."

"I'm not nosy. Just curious.

An expression covered John Wayne's face that Matt could not define. Was it reverie? Was it pain? Was it an emotion of searching for something irretrievably lost?

"She was the second love of my life. Anna. Her name was Anna." He fell silent, and the inscrutable expression returned to his face. Matt did not interrupt whatever was tugging at his new-found friend's emotions. After several minutes of quiet, John spoke again.

"She was one of my graduate students. A good bit younger than me. I should have known better, but I let myself fall in love with her. She graduated in May; we married in June." John paused again. Matt wondered at John's ability and willingness to open up to a stranger. Matt had seen something beyond intriguing in the philosopher. He saw something admirable, something of value, something that he wanted to glean from John.

"We were together a long time, happily together. After a time of the sweetest love a man could know, I fell into a habit of going to work and coming home to my room while she spent her time alone. I knew she was missing me, but I couldn't help myself. There is something compelling about knowing, and I found myself obsessively wanting to know.

"I began to find more and more interest in my books, my writing, my hours alone in thought. That's about the time she decided she wanted to be a trial lawyer. She passed the bar in record time and became one of the most successful defense lawyers in the region. Her life became more vibrant, more exciting than sitting at home with a philosopher who was there but gone." John paused again. The expression on his face intensified. He seemed engrossed in thoughts of something he could not quite grasp. Matt waited silently until John was ready to continue.

"I let her get away, barrister. I loved her with all my heart, and she loved me. But like the enchanting calls of sirens to mariners of old, the lure of life and living pulled her away."

"I'm sorry to hear that, John. I can tell you really loved her." Matt paused and the men sat silent for a long time. Finally, Matt broke the silence. "I know a woman I want you to meet." Matt thought of Miss Florence.

"No. I've ruined the lives of two women in my time. That's enough."

"Do you want to tell us about the other one?"

"No, I don't," John stood up. "I've got to get back to my people at the overpass. Some of them will be needing money for lunch, and it's getting late."

"You have money to buy food for your friends?"

"On the fifteenth of each month, an anonymous cash transfer in my name shows up at the mission. They hold the money until I need it. I never need much, so the rest goes to help my friends—my neighbors, I should say."

Matt stared at John in disbelief. What could motivate a man to give his money away and live under a bridge? How could anyone be that selfless? How could anyone be happy in that position? He had to ask the question.

"I am not particularly happy, barrister, but I do have joy

and there is a difference. Happiness is an event. It's when you greet a loved one after a long absence, or the sound of a child's laughter, or insight into a profound truth you have not seen before; joy is a satisfied feeling that all is well with your soul, and you are where you want and need to be."

Matt had to know the answer to another question. "Who sends the money?"

"I don't know. Mission workers will only tell me they have been sworn to secrecy. So the money keeps coming, and I keep helping my friends—and myself. I get for myself the few things I need. Of course, the little Social Security check—that I've tried to reject and they keep on sending the third of every month—comes too. I didn't ask for it. Never have. They make me take it. They said I needed it in order to pay for Medicare. Don't need that either. Don't ever use it."

"You never see a doctor?"

"No." John paused for a moment in thought. "I guess I should see a doctor about my prostate. When I go—and I go a lot—it seems like I'm peeing through the eye of a needle. Other times when I start, it's like turning on the spray of a shower head."

"You need to see about it, John. That condition could be serious."

"No. No use in crowding the over-worked doctor's offices. I'll leave my space to patients with serious illnesses like heart disease and cancer. I'm doing fine." Silence once more settled on the group.

Matt felt a need to verbalize a thought nagging him since John's revelation about the monthly checks. He broke the silence.

"John, do you realize that you could have a home?"

"I have a home, and you have been a guest in it." John thought for a moment then added, "Perhaps I should say you've been a guest at it."

They arrived at the overpass. Before John got out of the car, Matt asked, "Are you sure you don't know where the money comes from?"

"Perhaps so; perhaps not. See you around, barrister. Thanks for the lunch." John walked away in his usual gliding stride.

Troubled, Matt drove slowly back to Tybee. Along the way, he asked himself over and over how could a man be driven to give up personal comfort and physical well-being because of the loss of a woman, and why would anyone throw away creature ease and a bank account for any reason?

He had forgotten the question he meant to ask of John. Questions in his own life suddenly seemed trivial and insignificant by comparison to others. He would have to give some thought to the philosopher's odd approach to peace and tranquility. Was the old man daft, or was he on to something?

# Six

*M*att slid the key into the lock and opened the door of his office just as the phone rang. He rushed to answer it. Maybe a paying client would be on the line. After all, the only case so far on the island, not only did not pay, but cost him ninety-seven dollars. He lifted the receiver.

"Ryan Law Firm, Matt Ryan speaking." He felt his pomposity a little foolish, but what the heck. He could be as important as he wanted to be on Tybee.

The voice on the other end asked, "May I speak with the senior partner please?" Matt immediately recognized Melody's voice.

"OK. You caught me. I must now offer you a margarita as payment for that misguided moment that I felt a little playful with my title."

"No thanks. I'm not in the mood. But I do want to see you tonight. I want to show you something. Can you come by about seven-thirty?"

Matt considered declining the invitation. Then he thought, what the heck. He would see Melody for a short while and then come home to an early bed. "All right, seven-thirty it is."

"See you then." The phone went silent and Melody apparently returned to her nursing duties.

Matt picked up the area phone book and thumbed through the pages, looking for a name that he may recognize as Carolyn's husband. He was sure it started with a W and if he saw it, maybe it would jog his memory. He scanned the names in the W section but nothing jumped out at him. He laid the phone book aside and turned on the TV. He stared indifferently at the screen until the evening news came on. When the program ended, he turned off the TV and locked the office door. As he turned toward Tybrisa Street and home, he noticed again the familiar young girl across the street on the corner looking his way. Before he made the turn at his corner, he looked into the girl's face. He guessed her age at about sixteen or seventeen. The girl smiled and he nodded.

Walking down Tybrisa, he turned his head to look over his shoulder at the sound of squealing car tires. He caught a quick glimpse of the girl alone in a Ford Mustang convertible wheeling onto Butler Avenue headed west toward Savannah. A brief surge of apprehension swept over him. He had heard that Southern women could sometimes be unpredictable. What was this particular one up to? He couldn't imagine any affront he had committed. Why was it him that she seemed to be focused on?

At his condo he pushed the girl out of his mind and freshened up a bit. He changed into walking shorts and a T-shirt.

At Melody's apartment he knocked on the door, and she appeared wearing a blue T-shirt bearing a logo that read "Save the Turtles," and medium length white shorts. She closed the door behind her and took Matt's hand.

"Come with me. I'm going to show you a couple of the most beautiful sights on the island." They walked down Chatham Avenue and turned left onto Fisherman's Walk and ascended the steps to the fishing pier. They passed the palmettos and wild lantana blanketing mounds of sand on each side of the pier. They stopped and Matt asked, "What now?" Melody pointed to the sun setting above the pines on Little Tybee and the Spanish Hammock peninsula to the west.

"Stand still and look that way." Melody pointed across Back River. They watched the sun tap dancing gingerly on the tops of the tallest trees. In what seemed like a few seconds, a portion of the sun sank below the skyline and began turning a bright orange. A short while later, the orange turned a dark red like a coal-fired furnace. In increments of discerning inches, the sun disappeared below trees outlined against the horizon, leaving a pink glow on cumulus clouds lounging almost motionless above the pines.

"That was a breathtaking sight, as remarkable as the aurora up on my end of the planet."

"That was only half the show. There's something else I want you to see." Melody took Matt's hand and the couple walked down the river and around the curve onto the beach. They walked north toward the pavilion and pier.

Walking past the little grove of palms where they had previously made love, Matt felt an urgent stirring spreading through his lower abdomen. For a moment he thought of guiding Melody to that spot, but then he thought how unfair that would be when his heart was set on finding Carolyn.

Melody, too, remembered the night near the palm grove on the sand with Matt. She looked up at him and smiled then giggled self-consciously. She took Matt's hand and tugged him along behind her.

"I know what you are thinking, but no, no." She held onto his hand until they reached the pier. They ascended the steps and walked several feet along the rough-hewn boards. They stopped, and Melody guided Matt to a spot facing unusually calm surf. They stood side by side looking out over the gentle ocean. Night began to fall, and when darkness enveloped them, Melody pointed to the east. "Look right over there."

Matt focused his attention in the direction Melody indicated. In a few minutes, a fire began to blaze red on the water. They watched the full moon ascend in perceptible inches out of the ocean and continue to climb, turning bright orange and then yellow as it rose. An hour later a silvery glow shimmered high above the ocean.

"Wasn't that a breathtaking sight?" she asked Matt without looking at him. At that moment she found the view before her too compelling to turn away.

"I guess so, but I've seen the Atlantic before, you know. I lived on Long Island before I came here."

"No, silly. The moonrise. Have you ever seen anything as gorgeous as that?"

Matt gazed out over the ocean for a long while. "As a matter of fact, maybe I haven't. I've never paid much attention to stars and planets and stuff like that. I guess I've never had time for such things."

"Well, you've got time now. On Tybee, the time is whatever you want it to be—unless you are a nurse and you have to be at work by seven."

Matt looked down into Melody's face. He felt an urge to take her in his arms and hold her close, to absorb some of her innocence, her honesty, her familiarity and comfort with the world around her. Her sweetness was contagious, and he suddenly realized his admiration for her was deeper than any he had ever felt for anyone, even his high school baseball coach. "We'd better go," he said and took Melody's arm and led her down the pier. "You have to make that early shift in the morning."

Before they reached the pavilion, Melody stopped and turned to face Matt.

"There's something I've wanted to tell you since our first night on the beach. I don't know why I let you go that far that night. Maybe it wasn't you; maybe it was me. But that's the first time I've ever let myself go that far so early in a relationship. It just somehow seemed the right thing to do." She paused and circled her arms around Matt's waist and laid her head against his chest. Matt wrapped his arms around her, feeling the warmth of her body and inhaling the lilac fragrance of her hair. He laid his cheek atop her head, and they stood silent for a long time.

Melody nestled her head against his chest and pulled his body closer to hers. "I'm not going to give you a history of my sexual experience because it's none of your business. But I will say that it has been very limited and not at all impressive in any sense of the word."

"You are right. That's none of my business, and I would not ask you about it. And I agree with your assessment of our first night together. It seemed right." At that moment Matt felt a strange familiarity with Melody that left him puzzled and confused. It seemed that he had known her forever. But he did not welcome the feeling. He had another mission to accomplish that did not include the woman so warm and currently present in his arms.

"Well anyway, for what it's worth, I just wanted you to know that." Melody released her embrace and the couple walked from the pavilion to her apartment without further speaking.

At her door Matt kissed her lightly near the corner of her mouth and walked into the night. *What has that one night of lust gotten me into?* was his last thought before finally falling asleep sometime after midnight.

# Seven

$\mathcal{M}$att opened his office as usual around ten the next morning. He read the *Tybee Breeze* and the *Savannah Morning News* and waited for the phone to ring. By twelve it was still silent, so he decided to go into town and see if John Wayne and Robert would have lunch with him. At the overpass he found the philosopher in his usual place reading a book. He looked up when Matt approached.

"Well, top o' the morning to you, barrister. I didn't expect to see you so soon. What have you gotten yourself into now?"

"What makes you think I'm into something?"

"Just a hunch, barrister. You look guilty."

"Well, there is something I want to talk to you about. Can I do that over lunch?"

"Sure. If you are buying."

"Why should I pay? I picked up the tab last time—including the tip." Matt intended to buy lunch. After all, it was he who extended the invitation. He would not let the homeless old man or Robert pay even if John offered, even if he did support some of his homeless friends.

"You know the drill. It's your counseling session, barrister. For that you have to pay."

They drove several blocks and entered a restaurant on West Jones Street. The three diners ordered chili cheese dogs and exchanged the usual pleasantries. When the meals were set before them, Matt broached the question he came to ask the philosopher.

"I didn't tell you this before, but one of the reasons I came to Savannah was to find a woman. I still need to do that, but I met another girl, a wonderful person. There's only one thing wrong: she's not my type."

"I don't know what that means," John responded, "but we'll get to that later. Do you have feelings for this new girl?"

"I think so, but I'm not sure."

"This other woman, the one you are looking for, do you think of her when you are with the new girl?"

"What do you mean, when I'm with her? Do you mean when I'm talking with her, when I'm walking hand in hand with her, or when we are intimate?"

"Intimate. That's your first mistake. How long did you know this girl before that happened?"

"Couple hours."

"So this was a one night stand that got out of control, grabbed you and wouldn't let go?"

"Well, sort of. She was a one night stand, and I think I can get over her, but I'm not sure I want to."

"You lied to me, barrister. You said you weren't in a mess. You are in a ton of it. But let's get back to the question. Does this new woman make you forget the one you came looking for?"

Matt thought for a moment. "I don't think so, at least not entirely. But there's something about her that I've never experienced before in anyone. There's a trusting, honest, completeness about her that I admire and can't shake. And she's in love with me."

"Did she tell you that?"

"No."

"Then how do you know, barrister?"

"I just know it. I can feel it. A man knows when he is loved. A woman doesn't. She has to be told, and we don't understand why she doesn't know. We mow the lawn, open jars, and pat her on the butt when we pass her in the hallway. We love, support, and nurture her children, love and tolerate her mother, and even pretend to love her cat. That's the way we constantly express our love, but she just doesn't get it."

"True enough." John rubbed his chin and asked, "Did the other woman make you feel loved?"

"Yes." Matt thought for a moment then qualified his answer. "Well, not exactly. Not all the time. But we were young and I loved her."

"But you let her get away."

"Yes I did. And I want her back."

"And she belongs to another now?"

"Carolyn, that's her name. And yes, she is married. Melody is not, and she is in love with me. Is it right that I want both of them?"

"'Right' is a tricky concept, barrister. We are not born into a reality of rightness and wrongness, you know. We don't have a clue about what we are doing here on this planet. Reality must be created. The way we do that is through love of family, love of our fellow man, and humility before our creator. Is that something we all can do? Maybe so; maybe not. But that's what we try to do. We take breath, motility, and wisdom and mold them into what is perceived as right. Is perception always right? Sometimes yes; sometimes no. There was a time when women and minorities lacked the good sense to vote, a time when abortion was wrong, a time when it was unethical for journalists to out a president who had temporarily slipped the bonds of faithful matrimony. Right has a way of changing. Is it reasonable to assume, therefore, that absolute right does not exist?"

"I don't know, but if right does not exist,  I can create my own rules?"

"You've studied and practiced law, barrister. You know better than that. We look to family, to culture, to institutions, and to traditions to arrive at cultural truth, societal truth, legal truth, not your truth."

"You started out being fun. Now you've ruined it."

"It is what it is, barrister. You've heard that statement before. It's not a Yogi-ism. It's true."

"Is that absolute truth?'

"It's my truth at this particular time, barrister. Get over it."

The three diners finished their meal. The temperature outside had risen to the middle nineties, and the conversation was going well, so they decided to stay inside and have a beer. The waiter sat the drinks before them. After taking a long swallow, John spoke.

"I mentioned to you once a second woman's life I have messed up. Let me tell you about her." He leaned back in his seat and formed a triangle with his thumbs and index fingers.

"Her name was Angelica. We began school together. At recess we played together, and I always knew I felt something glorious, something wonderful inside when I was near her or when I thought of her—and yes, when later I began to dream of her. It wasn't until junior high that I realized that feeling was love. It was then that we declared that love and began a courtship that lasted until that terrible day she told me she was pregnant." John paused and looked down at his hands. After an extended moment, he clasped his hands tightly together as if trying to hold on to something slipping away. Matt remained silent, anticipating something remarkable. John stared at his hands clasped on the table and continued the story.

"You would think at this point I would be overjoyed, and I would have—if the baby had been mine."

Matt stared at the philosopher and gulped a quick breath through his suddenly opened mouth. Robert turned his head sharply and looked at his friend.

John seemed to not notice their reaction and continued the story.

"All through high school, she hinted in every way—and even joked sometimes—that she wanted more than hugs and kisses. But as I told you before, I came from a conservative family in a conservative town. Sex was something for marriage and children. My parents raised me to believe that, and I did." John paused, blinked several times, and continued.

"She had the baby, a beautiful boy, and gave him away. It wasn't until later when she was in the fourth stage of cervical cancer that I knew the full story. I was holding her hand when she took her last weak breath. Before she died, she told me of her urgent need for me all through high school. That's when I knew I had killed her. I was so naïve and indoctrinated in conservatism that I could not see or understand her needs. She began to satisfy those needs in other places.

"After the baby came, she continued her promiscuous behavior with many different men. From that experience with Angelica, I learned first-hand that the world is not always what it seems. I matured, and that's when I discovered the difference between social conservatives and social liberals. Liberals just live their lives. She lived her life, and at the end of the day, I'm glad she did. I'm glad she lived a little and did not waste her short life waiting for me." John grew silent and sat up straight for a few seconds then leaned on his forearms on the table. He picked up the beer bottle and took three successive swallows. After each swallow he stared at the bottle as if seeking answers to obscure questions in his mind. He sat the bottle on the table and spoke again.

"It was in that last confession that she told me things I will have to live with the rest of my life. After what she told me, I wanted to go to hell, but I couldn't. Hell is where I belonged, but my conservatism would not allow me to take my own life. She told me that with every man she slept with from high school on she pretended it was me. She didn't say this, and I knew she didn't want me to think this, but at that moment I realized she was seeking to satisfy her need for me with all those other men. The series of multiple lovers at a young age contributed to the cancer and it killed her." At this revelation, John fell silent for a long moment, and the oppressive atmosphere enveloping the trio turned heavier as if multiple canisters of tear gas had suddenly exploded in the room.

"So you see, barrister, I'm no good for women."

"But you married later?"

"Yes I did. Anna was so beautiful, so perfect, and so persistent. I'm glad I did. We had some good years together. Anna is the only woman I've ever had. But she was energetic and adventurous, and our relationship was wonderful. Wonderful and wild. With her I enjoyed every woman in the world." John paused. His eyes began a quiet sparkle. Subtle smile lines took up residence at the corners of his eyes and mouth. It was obvious that he was reminiscing.

"By the way, gentlemen, I later learned that Angelica's doings were not the only goings on in my town. I grew up thinking mine was like the town I read about once that was so bland and uneventful that when their mayor died, the headline in the weekly newspaper read, Mayor Dead at 83. The next week's headline, still with nothing to report, read Mayor Still Dead at 83."

The three men laughed at John's little joke and the atmosphere turned lighter. He had accomplished his goal.

"Jesus was a social and economic liberal, y'all know," John said after the laugh. Robert, still laughing made no response.

"No, I didn't know that," Matt replied.

"Read your Bible, barrister. It's all in there."

# Eight

On the drive back to Tybee Island, Matt pondered over and over his conversation with John. He was more confused now than before. Was he—like John—not good for women? His dilemma had taken on a new sense of urgency. Should he continue the search for Carolyn or cultivate a closer relationship with Melody? He decided to approach the question in the way he thought the philosopher would. He considered the issue from every angle. Arriving at the island, he realized he was still unable to make a decision. He was not ready to give up the search for Carolyn and the possibility of reconnecting with her, nor was he ready to end his relationship with Melody.

He continued to see her often, but never attempted intimacy with her, even though he knew she was available. He continued a perfunctory search for Carolyn, still apprehensive about confronting her. In mid-August he chanced upon a promising lead in an unexpected place. He opened the *Savannah Morning News* on a Sunday and there it was: an advertisement for the Winston State Bank, Carolyn Winston, President. That was it! Now he remembered. Her husband was J. Randolph Winston. But if Carolyn was now the president, where was her husband? Matt imagined several scenarios. Their marriage had not worked out and now they were divorced, and she had taken old J. Randolph to the cleaners. Serves him right. These May-December relationships never work out and the old fools are left holding the bag, the empty bag. He smiled inwardly at that thought, and again it crossed his mind that perhaps old J. Randolph was dead or maybe in a nursing home. After all, he was already old when Carolyn married him.

A scattering of unremarkable legal cases had begun coming to his office, and after he had taken care of them the next morning, he decided to pay a visit to the Winston State Bank. He didn't know what he would do if he saw Carolyn. And worst of all, what would she do if she saw and recognized him? What would be her attitude? Would she be forgiving? Would she be vengeful? Would she humiliate him in front of customers and bank employees?

Matt's eagerness to see Carolyn overcame the trepidation he felt and he drove into Savannah. In the parking lot of the Winston State Bank, he sat in his car formulating in his mind what he would say if he confronted Carolyn. Should he act nonchalant? Should he offer to hug her? What if he reached for her and she turned away? He breathed a deep breath and opened the car door and walked slowly to the bank. Inside, a dozen customers stood in line at teller stations. Three bank officers sat at desks serving patrons seeking loans or carrying out other business. Matt stood at a display table pretending to examine brochures. Unobtrusively as possible he scanned the large bank lobby. He saw no one he recognized as Carolyn. He turned to leave and a tall dark-haired woman stepped through an office door and walked to one of the seated bank officers. She placed a manila folder on the desk and bent down to speak quietly near the seated woman's right ear. Carolyn straightened and looked into Matt's face. Her gaze remained focused on his eyes for a long moment then scanned up and down the full length of his body. A look of surprise flashed quickly across her face then faded. She turned briskly and disappeared into the office from which she had previously emerged.

Did she recognize him? Did she know it was him and refused to acknowledge him? The expression on her face clearly demonstrated her interest. But what was it? Was it physical fascination? Did she know it was him she was staring at and unsure of how she should react?

Matt left the bank with all these thoughts running through his mind at a feverish pace. On the drive back to Tybee, he determined that no matter what, he had to see her and talk to her. Maybe he could call her on the phone, or send an e-mail to the address he found on one of the bank's brochures, or perhaps he could go to the bank and ask to see the president. But what about J. Randolph? Matt had had enough presence of mind to check Carolyn's left hand and there was no ring. But that did not answer definitively the question of the whereabouts of her husband.

Matt reached the island and drove around the Inlet Avenue circle at the Park of the Seven Flags and pointed his car west on Butler Avenue. As he drove past Tybrisa Street, the girl from the corner stepped out of a bar and waved and smiled at the passing Mercedes. Matt looked at the girl, but did not respond. He parked in front of his office. Absent mindedly, his thoughts still swirling around the sighting of Carolyn, he turned the key in the lock and walked inside. He went to close the door and found it obstructed. He looked up to see the young girl from the corner pushing her way inside.

"Can I help you, young lady?" Matt asked.

"Maybe you can. I need a beer and they wouldn't sell me one at the bar over there. Everybody always wants to see my ID card. Can you believe that?"

Matt took a seat behind his desk. The girl did have somewhat of a mature look about her, but she couldn't possibly be more than sixteen or seventeen. "Of course I can. You're too young to buy beer. You're too young to drink beer. How old are you? Sixteen?"

"I'm older than you think. I'm old enough for you."

"I don't think so. I'm old enough to be your father."

"That's OK. I need a daddy. Mine died three years ago."

"I'm sorry. But you need to look elsewhere for a father, young lady. I'm not him."

"You could be. My mother is not married—well, actually

she's not my mother, but anyway, she's not married whatever she is."

Matt inhaled a deep breath. He was learning more than he needed to know about this girl. "I'm sorry about all your domestic problems, young lady, but I think you should go."

Matt stood up to escort the intruder from his office. The phone rang and he lifted the receiver and returned to his chair.

While he talked on the phone, the girl moved across the room and sat on the side of Matt's desk. He surveyed her long, deeply-tanned legs emerging from blue shorts. With reluctant effort he forced his gaze from her legs but could not ignore the sight of her tight, tanned belly below a red halter top. He forced his gaze from her body to her long, dark hair. Suddenly he became aware of how tall she was and felt a vague sense of recognition of a past lover. The conversation ended and Matt returned the phone to its cradle.

The girl looked at Matt and said, "I need a job. Don't you need a secretary? I've worked before, you know. Waited tables at a steakhouse in town—two thirteen an hour plus tips and all the peanuts I could eat. They served alcohol, and when they found out my real age, *phfft* I was history." Matt knew in his heart that he needed to get the girl out of his office, but her presence and free spirit fascinated and hypnotized him.

"I can answer the telephone and file papers away and stuff. I work cheap, two thirteen an hour and I won't even ask for peanuts." The girl smiled through gleaming white teeth and pink lips. Matt also had to chuckle. His smile quickly faded when the girl suddenly lay back on the desk, slipped off her sandals, and pumped her legs high in the air. She looked up at Matt and smiled. "I can provide other services, too."

"Young lady, I'm an attorney familiar with all the laws of the land. Do you realize that what you are suggesting—even if I were willing to go along with you, which I'm not—could land me in a Georgia prison for a long time?"

"Marry me then. We could go over to South Carolina today and fix it all up. Then it would be legal."

The girl's suggestion shocked Matt into the realization that he had entertained her much too long. It was time to put an end to her foolishness. He took her arm and lifted her to her feet. He waited while she slipped her feet into her sandals then ushered her to the door. He opened it and the girl reached into a pocket of her shorts and pulled out a piece of paper.

"Here. Call me." Matt brushed the offer away, and the note dropped to the floor. The girl  pranced onto the sidewalk laughing.

"If you come back or stalk me again, young lady, I'll have you arrested," Matt called after her. She pirouetted on her toes like a winged princess, and laughing loudly, gave Matt a finger gesture with both hands.

Matt watched her disappear around the corner. He closed the door and picked up the paper from the floor. He intended to throw it in the waste basket beside his desk, but the striking penmanship on the note caught his attention. He looked at it and read "Princess" and a phone number. He dropped the note into the trash basket and returned to the chair behind his desk. He stretched out his legs and leaned back in the chair. Looking up at the ceiling, he thought, *damn, why do I have to be thirty-five? Wait till the philosopher hears about this.*

# Nine

*M*att spent the next few weeks interacting with, John, Robert, Florence, and Melody. He still had not initiated intimacy with her again, even though she made it clear in not-so-subtle nuances that she was ready for more than occasional hugs and passionless kisses now and then. Neither had he made further progress in his need to approach Carolyn. He was a former corporate lawyer who had gone against some of the toughest men and corporations in New York and beyond. That meant nothing now in his current quest. He could not get past his fear of confronting her. He visited her bank several times and lounged in the lobby until he could catch a glimpse of her. The security guard began watching him closely and finally asked if he were going to conduct business. Matt stammered something about looking to transfer his banking affairs. After that spontaneous statement, he thought of how appropriate was his choice of words and smiled inwardly. But business was not the "banking affair" he had in mind. Following that incident with the bank guard, he decided to lay low before he was arrested, or worse, attract the attention of the bank president.

The Sunday before Labor Day 2011 came, and Melody persuaded Matt to meet her for the morning worship service on the Pavilion. That achievement, which did not come easy, encouraged her to coax him into attending the island fireworks display that night. Not given to attending such events, he found himself caught up in the excitement and exuberance, along with other locals, tourists, and day trippers from miles around, and began to enjoy the festivities.

Weeks passed and Matt still had not contacted Carolyn, but he was determined to make a move soon.

Meanwhile, Melody invited him to join her for the annual October Tybee Pirates Fest. She dressed herself and Matt in full pirate apparel, and with makeup bought from the local vendor, she soon had Matt looking a little like Johnny Depp as he appeared in his pirate movies.

Pirates Charles, a six piece band from California, played beneath the big tent on the beach. The couple danced almost every dance, Matt drinking beer between sets, Melody sipping wine. Before the day and evening ended, Matt had downed more beer than he intended. Twilight descended and he struggled to walk a straight line and see everything he should see. But he did see Melody. And with every cup of beer, his memory of their first night together, how beautiful she was, and how warm and willing she presented herself became clearer in his mind.

"Let's go for a walk on the beach to help you clear your head," she said to Matt as they stood in the center of the Tybee Island traffic circle, watching the frivolity of the crowds and listening to music from Tybrisa Street. Matt looked at his watch.

"It's almost nine. Some of the restaurants will be closing soon. Let's get a bite. Then we can take a walk after dinner." Matt did not want to go to the beach. He feared his reaction, especially if they neared the palm grove where they had spent their first night together. The sea breeze had turned cool, but if they chose to, they could generate their own warmth on the sand.

They walked up Tybrisa Street and made a right turn onto Butler past the crowded bars on the corner. They decided to walk up to North Beach for dinner. The longer Matt walked, the clearer his mind became and the straighter his step.

They entered the restaurant and placed their order. Over dinner, with nothing in particular to talk about, Matt asked Melody a series of questions about the island and its people. He had made a point of acquainting himself with the area and began to vicariously learn about the island's colorful evolution, and Melody loved to talk about her home town.

"Our little island is about five miles long and a football field or two wide, except for the vast marsh. The small size may be the reason some tourists occasionally get a little crazy, and could be the reason they seem to enjoy it so much. We are about the size of a major park, and the beach is mostly what we are. We are eighteen miles east of the Savannah mainland.

"Depending on how you want to look at it, U.S. Highway 80 ends—or begins—at the Park of the Seven Flags. Standing in the park and facing west, it is fun to imagine the course of the highway to San Diego, and the stories told and the stories yet to be told along the three thousand mile route. Most islanders—me included—would argue with very strong conviction that all roads eventually connect in some way with U.S.80 and end at Tybee Island. Once here, who would care where it goes? Nobody wants to leave anyway.

"We can get a little quirky here on the island. But that's the way we like it. It's a place where preachers and sinners work and live side by side. My preacher remarked in church once that this is the only place he had been where a member came into his office and used the same language he used with his friends in the street."

Matt couldn't help chuckling at that disclosure. He had already observed some of that. Melody smiled and did not miss a beat in talking about her island.

"This is the only place I know of where millionaires and just-getting-byers interact without even the slightest acknowledgment of their differences. We all share a kinship and mutual respect from knowing that we possess a home grander than any other place on earth. Like all towns, counties, and cities, though, there is an elite clique here. But on Tybee the clique is so small nobody notices.

"A little over three thousand permanent residents live on the island, and a few families choose to forego the quirk and live lives like those found in any typical suburb or rural town. But most of us prefer the quirk, and the others still live in harmony with the rest of us and think of all islanders as brothers and sisters.

"Savannah, Tybee and the other barrier islands, welcome tourists from all over the nation and the world. We love to see visitors come and enjoy our home like we do."

The couple finished their meal and began the walk back to South Beach. Melody continued talking along the way, and Matt listened without interrupting.

"Locals and visitors alike form various opinions of our tiny island. *Southern Living* and *Outside* magazines called it a 'best beach.' *Family Fun* magazine described Tybee as a place of 'unhurried pace and charm of the South, a place where kids still ride their bikes everywhere.' *Conde Nast Traveler* magazine said our beach is a place of 'more sun for less money,' and named Savannah 'one of the top ten travel destinations' and declared the city 'a work of art.' *USA Today* named the Savannah waterfront 'one of the top ten.' I am so proud of those kudos.

"In the metropolitan area, we have some of the best chefs in the country, most certainly some of the best in the South. Everybody everywhere knows the Paula Deen family. And one of our Tybee Island chefs bears the title of "one of the best cooks in America." He served the John F. Kennedy, Jr./Carolyn Bessette wedding on Cumberland Island, a little ways down the coast south of Tybee.

"Writers and observers from all around seem to enjoy stating opinions about the island. One writer referred to it with the tongue-in-cheek expression 'A drinking island with a fishing problem.' We love our little island and take all of this in stride.

"You have probably read the tag line of the author regularly writing in the *Tybee Breeze*, 'If you are lucky enough to live on Tybee, you are lucky enough.'

"Another observer likes to say, 'A bad day on Tybee beats any day anywhere else.'

"A movie maker filming *The Last Song* on Tybee a couple of years ago said of the island, 'The Georgia locations are handsome and the people are pretty, but any resemblance to real life is coincidental.'

"One writer playfully tagged the island "Redneck Riviera," an oxymoron for sure. Unlike the Riviera, though, elegance and opulence are rare finds here. And the term "redneck" generally refers to the ultra-conservative, uneducated, and bigoted. But most Tybee residents come from other places near and far, and the general attitude is one of worldly sophistication and toleration, but with no need to flaunt either quality. We like to paddle our own kayaks and let everyone else paddle theirs. Everybody has a place."

The couple stopped at 14$^{th}$ street and waited for the red light to change. Traffic had thinned out and the waiting was unnecessary, but neither Matt nor Melody felt a need to hurry. The light changed and they continued walking. Melody returned to her story of Tybee.

"We're different from most of the East Coast. Access to our five miles of beaches is unencumbered by high rises, hotels, and other obstructions. You don't have to walk through a building or someone's back yard to get to the sea.

"The island sits at the western tip of a cove along the Georgia shoreline between Florida and South Carolina, and the Gulf Stream—located about seventy-five miles off shore—helps steer winds northward. A perpetual summer-time Bermuda high creates a barrier between us and storms. These are the main reasons that for more than a century the island has escaped the hurricanes plaguing most of the eastern coastline and Gulf.

"The last seriously damaging hurricane to strike the area was in 1897, ten years after the town of 'Tybee Beach' was incorporated. The entire island, except for one dwelling, was blown or washed away by that storm. David, a category one hurricane, came ashore in 1979 with no more damage than minor flooding and a loosed shingle or two.

"The Bermuda high is a godsend to Tybee and the Georgia Coast. A mound of air eight miles high and one-to-two thousand miles wide rotates clockwise—opposite the movement of hurricanes, you know—near the island of Bermuda in the summer time. These winds usually steer storms away from Tybee. When the high shifts east, storms rotate around the air mass and move north of the Georgia coastline. A westward shift forces storms in that direction and southward, usually toward Florida and the Gulf of Mexico.

"The strength of the high largely determines the tracks of hurricanes. Strong Bermuda highs push storms toward the Southern U.S. coastline. Weak pressures guide them into the Northeast U.S. and Canada. But if luck holds, storms track into the cold waters of the North Atlantic and fizzle out."

Melody continued her monolog of the history and geography of the island until she and Matt reached the palm grove. Neither seemed aware that they were edging closer and closer to the place Matt wanted to avoid. But before he knew it, he found himself lying against a sand dune with Melody at his side. She turned toward Matt and nestled her head against his chest. She placed an arm across him and began stroking his stomach and chest with gentle movements of her nurse's hands. She moved her lips close to Matt's ear and continued her story of Tybee.

"In the distant past, Tybee and Savannah were favorite hangouts for pirates and vagabonds of every description. Tybee was somewhat isolated, and the ocean provided a quick escape route if needed. Local legend has it that Robert Louis Stephenson visited the area and fashioned Treasure Island after Tybee."

Melody paused in her monolog and snuggled closer to Matt's body. The night had turned cooler and their shared body warmth felt good. He turned his head and softly kissed her. She snuggled closer and laid a leg between his, her thigh pressing against his hip. He felt her leg lying softly against his groin. A stirring began in the region, and Matt thought of turning to face her and taking her firmly in his arms. But he was so warm and cozy where he lay with Melody's body softly against his he remained in place listening to her mesmerizing voice, impressed by her knowledge of her home.

"Some islanders will also swear that Captain Bluebeard's treasure is buried somewhere on North Beach."

She paused and kissed Matt on the cheek. He turned again and kissed her firmly on lips tasting like sweet wine. The kiss ended and the couple lay looking into each other's eyes. After a long moment of indecision, Matt turned away and gazed into the sky filled with early fall stars, the outer throes of the Milky Way clearly visible.

"It seems that the free-spiritedness of those pirate days survived somewhat with time. The region continued for a long period semi-isolated, accessible only by boat or train. Inhabitants often made their own rules and modified cultural traditions as time went on. I have heard it said that back in the 20s and 30s, Tybee was the place to be for partying and gambling. Partying, as you have seen, is still a favorite pastime on the island. This attitude and behavior helped earn for the city and county the grandiose title of 'The Great State of Chatham.'"

Melody raised her upper body and leaned over Matt and pressed her lips to his. The soft kiss turned urgent and Melody pressed harder against him. Several seconds passed and Matt opened his eyes and lifted Melody from his chest. He laid her on the soft, moist sand and returned to his place against the dune and closed his eyes. With Melody's body lying against his and her soft voice against his ear, he felt calm and contented.

A short while later, he fell into a deep sleep. Dreams of Carolyn began to mingle with the alcohol and spread like dawning sunlight into his mind. They were law students at Harvard. The first season blizzard was howling outside, and classes were canceled for the day. And after the loving, they lay warm, flushed, and contented. They closed their eyes and listened to the wind hum a soft tune beneath the eaves of the dormitory, and Matt turned on his side and gently fondled both of Carolyn's breasts simultaneously with one hand.

# Ten

$\mathcal{M}$att awoke to early morning coolness in the sand and sun casting soft shadows beneath the trees in the palm grove. He sat up and looked at Melody lying on her back, sound asleep with her hands folded beneath her breasts. He stared at her face for a minute, maybe longer. He didn't want to disturb her, and he could not bring himself to turn away from that compelling vision.

She opened her eyes and stretched her arms above her head and yawned. She smiled at Matt and lifted a hand to caress his face.

"You ready to get up?" He asked in a low voice.

"I guess we should. What time is it?"

"I don't know. I hope you don't have duty at the hospital today."

"No. My next shift is scheduled for Wednesday."

"Well I do," Matt lied. I'm working on a project I need to finish in a hurry. We'll get some breakfast, and I'll walk you home.

After a long breakfast with multiple cups of warming coffee, Matt and Melody walked down Butler to Inlet Avenue and to her apartment. They shared a gentle kiss, and Matt went home for a shower and change of clothes. It was Sunday, but Matt went to his office in case Melody would be checking up on him—which she did not.

He read the front page and the sports section of the *Savannah Morning News*. He thought of John Wayne and Robert and remembered that none of the missions serve lunch on Sunday. Maybe he should go into town and take them to lunch.

He locked his office and walked to his condo. He started his car and drove west toward Savannah. Driving along Islands Expressway, thoughts of how beautiful Melody looked in the soft dawn permeated his mind. He felt guilty about rejecting her last night. She clearly wanted him, and he had to admit he also wanted her. But that would have been grossly unfair with another woman in his subconscious mind dominating his dreams through the night.

He neared the Truman overpass and saw John and Robert walking up Islands Expressway. The shoulder of the road was too narrow to stop, so he drove to the driveway of an abandoned building on the right near the Broad Street intersection. The two men walked to where Matt waited and explained that they were headed to Forsyth Park where the Christian Church was serving lunch, a practice of every Sunday.

"How about a sit-down lunch on River Street?" Matt asked. John looked at Robert, seeking his approval. Robert shrugged his shoulders in agreement.

"Sure. We can do that. That'll be two more meals for our friends at the park."

The two men got into Matt's car and the three of them drove the short distance to River Street. Over lunch Matt told the story of "Princess" and the proposition she had made.

"There she was spread out on my desk in perfect position for serious monkey business. Thoughts went through my mind. All I had to do was slip her shorts off. I could have easily locked my office door. No one was expected anyway. But I couldn't do something like that with a child no matter how experienced or willing she was."

"You don't need to feel guilty. Lust in men is universal and sure," John interjected. "That's the way God made us. Go forth and multiply, he said. Then he injected us with testosterone to make sure we follow his command. Even the most spiritual among us in civilized society wrestle with these feelings. You recall, of course, the politicians, preachers and scores of others who have taken this God-given gift too far. You remember the statement President Jimmy Carter made in a 1976 issue of *Playboy* magazine. He admitted to adultery many times in his heart. But Mr. Carter would never actually do that, of course. And he knew that for those 'transgressions' he was forgiven. It's almost impossible for a normal man not to appreciate an attractive woman of any age whether eighteen or a hundred and eighteen."

The three men sat silent for a while, letting the philosopher's declaration sink in. John took a long pull of sweet tea, and with a wry smile on his lips, he spoke.

"Maybe that young lady offered to marry you looking for an easy place to land. You know, when some women marry they are absolved of all future responsibilities. If their children turn out to be axe murderers, it's the husband's fault. If the children discover a cure for cancer, it's a direct result of the sacrifices the wife has made and the suffering she has endured in spite of the children's father." John chuckled and took another pull of sweet tea.

The other men chuckled also at John's little joke, then all were quiet until Robert broke the silence. He was a quiet man who hardly ever spoke unless he was spoken to. But words suddenly came tumbling from his mouth.

"My daddy was a truck driver," he began. "The summer I turned twelve and school was out, I asked him why he never took me and mama on some of his trips. With a straight face, he told me he could think of ten reasons not to take mama with him and only one why he should. Then he laughed and laughed like he had said the funniest thing ever spoke. Older kids at school had taught me enough to know what he was talking about. I hated my daddy even before he said that. He died two months later when me and mama caught him in a room at a truck stop with two strange women. Mama shot all three of them.

"I was there. I saw it all, and I was glad until they took my mama to prison. She didn't take too good to a cage and died after five years of a life sentence. I guess she completed all of her sentence like the judge told her to. They buried her in the prison cemetery.

"A juvenile detention facility was my home for the next thirteen months and five days. It was a fine home, a fine home indeed. Every weekend I was isolated by the part-time juvenile officer who had his way with me. By that I mean he had his way with me. He did things to me I wouldn't even describe to Jesus. His regular job was with the city of Chicago. I'll never forget that gay bastard. He was tall and skinny with a hatchet face that could fell one of these big, ancient Savannah live oaks with three whacks. His nose was like a woodpecker's beak, and he always had this contemptuous look on his face like he had walked into a crowded Mexican diner and everyone broke wind at the same time. 'Broke wind,' that's what John taught me to say instead of the word."

Matt thought of Michael Clark Duncan whose character was wrongfully executed in the Tom Hanks movie, *The Green Mile,* and the irony of Robert's physical resemblance to the actor, and the child's incarceration simply because he had no other place to go following his father's murder and his mother's conviction for the crime.

"When some men go to prison or into politics, they get religion. All I got was angry and bitter. They let me out of the youth development center in the custody of an aunt. She treated me OK till I graduated from high school and my state subsistence was cut. She got real mean then.

"I felt comfortable and safe at school. I loved everything about it and played basketball and football. I wanted to grow up to be somebody, and I worked hard and scored the best grades. I graduated with an A average, but even with that a decent job for a young black man was hard to come by. I went months without a job and things turned so bad at my aunt's I took to the streets.

"The day I turned twenty-one, I got my ID card and went to a bar just to prove I could. And low-and-behold, sitting at the bar was that sonofabitch that made me his weekend child bride. I knew what I had to do. No telling how many boys he had done that to. But I played it smart. I sat down beside him and ordered a beer just as normal as you please. We started a conversation, and after a little while I very quietly asked him if he was a child-molesting faggot piece of shit. I knew what he was going to do. He hit me and I deliberately fell off the bar stool. I hollered loud so everyone would notice. I let him pick me up and pound on me some more. With every blow, I pretended he was hurting me. But then he got in a good lick that broke and blooded my nose. That's when I let him have it. I hit him one time and his head smashed against the corner of the bar so hard it crushed his skull. He was dead before he could remember what he had done to me. I hated that part. I wanted him to remember real good.

"Witnesses testified in my defense, and the judge let me off with probation for involuntary manslaughter. I looked for work again after that, but of course the Chicago papers were full of the total event, from the crime to the trial to the verdict to the sentence. I went back to the streets for a long time, but I eventually figured out that I could do the same street gig in the warmer climes of South Georgia. Been here ever since.

"I grew up poor as an Iranian whore. My daddy made good money driving a truck, but me and mama never saw much of it. I tried hard, but I never got over all that, and then this other crap started falling on me. Other than my mama, I never connected with anybody, never had a real friend, never felt like I belonged. The only realities I've known were my mama, the women I've loved, and recognition of a higher power. Then I met John. He's got all this education and he knows just about everything. But he never looked down on me, never treated me different. That's why I take care of him. I will as long as I live."

John looked at Robert and smiled. "Or as long as I live, my friend. I'm a lot older than you, and age has a way of befriending death."

The men fell silent. A couple of minutes passed, and Robert seemed to be feeling discomfort at the silence and sentimentality.

He had to say something.

"Y'all been talking about women. Let me tell you what I think about them. I loved many women back in the day. But in every experience, I found it strange that a woman finds a man she thinks is perfect, and the first thing she does after he is hooked is start trying to change him. After that, both of them are in for nothing but frustration, 'cause he ain't gonna change, and she ain't gonna give up."

Matt and John didn't know how to respond. They couldn't tell whether Robert was serious or seeking only to break the silence with humor.

"Well one thing is for sure, gentlemen," John began. "This thing about men and women is precarious at best. We complain about them not understanding us, but you can rest assured they don't have a clue about what's going on with their man. We are manufactured differently, and that's the way it is and that's the way it always will be. There are lots more differences about us than what's going on down there. But to our credit, I truly believe we are more tolerant of those differences than they are.

"Think about it, in those heated disagreements that inevitably occur between the opposite genders, we are not the ones that run from the room in tears. We quite frequently end the dispute by agreeing, walking away, or shutting down. Now those behaviors themselves may be points of contention. That may end the verbal exchanges, but there is sufficient evidence to conclude that while the sound is no more, the fury goes on. It may sometimes go on infinitely. Women, I'm afraid, remember more efficiently than we do. They never forget, especially affronts. They keep mental and emotional lists. Now that, gentlemen, is knowledge you should remember."

"Damn, professor, you just gave me more information than I wanted," Matt said when John had finally concluded his dissertation.

"Me, too," Robert added.

No one spoke again on the short drive back to the overpass. When the two passengers got out of the car, John said quietly, "See you, barrister."

Matt offered a subtle wave of a hand, but said nothing. On the drive back to Tybee, his mind played over and over the story Robert told of the youthful abuse while incarcerated, and the killing in the bar, and the murder of his father and his lovers. Nothing else could possibly penetrate that heaviness. *What the hell have I got to complain about?* Matt thought.

# Eleven

On Monday morning Matt awoke to the ringing of the telephone. He checked the caller ID and saw that it was Melody. He ignored the call. The time had come to finally confront Carolyn. He got out of bed, dressed, and drove to his office. Ordinarily he would walk, but today he would go into town and approach her. He would come right out with his feelings. Lay it all out to her and let the chips fall. He had grown fatigued at procrastination he was not used to. He could no longer resist the urge to present himself to her and see what would happen. Even if she were married, he was resolved to fight like a hooked shark to get her back.

He drove to Savannah and pulled into the bank parking lot. He turned off the engine and sat for several minutes. He clutched the steering wheel and took a deep breath. When he gathered himself, he entered the bank and drifted toward a high table overladen with customer supplies. He picked up a few booklets and studied them then methodically returned each one to its proper place. He glanced around the room hoping to see Carolyn. He walked toward her office and approached a young woman sitting at a desk near the bank president's office door.

"May I see Mrs. Winston?"

"Maybe I can help you. What sort of business do you have?"

"It's something I need to see Mrs. Winston about. Can I see her?"

"Mrs. Winston left orders not to be disturbed. If I can't help you, you'll have to make an appointment and come back at another time." The woman's response was emphatic. *Rude,* Matt thought.

He gave her a long look and brushed quickly past her to the door marked Carolyn P. Winston, President. He opened the door and stuck his head inside.

"Knock, knock." The bank president looked up, obviously annoyed.

"May I help you?" she asked. *Curtly,* Matt thought.

"Can I come in?"

"No you may not. I'm very busy. You can see the lady outside my door."

"But I need to see you." Matt walked into the office.

Carolyn got up and walked around the corner of the desk. "Now look here, young man, I…. She stopped in midsentence and stood staring. After a few seconds, she asked, "Matt, is that you?"

"Yes it is. How have you been?"

Carolyn walked to the door and closed it. "Well! Matthew G. Ryan in the flesh. What brings you to Savannah?"

"All you have are questions? Not even a hug?"

"Do I owe you a hug, Matt?—or anything? You dumped me and ran off with French Whore. Is that why you deserve a hug?" Carolyn returned to her chair behind the desk.

"You owe me civility because I loved you—and you loved me." Matt paused for a moment, waiting for the next reaction from Carolyn. She glared at him, fury flashing in her darker than usual eyes.

"You loved me. Is that why you ran off with your rich French whore?"

"I'm sorry. Maybe that was a mistake. I realize now that I still love you. I've always loved you."

"Well, do you know what, Matt? I'm wealthy now, too, probably richer than your French whore. You want to know something else? I can have any man I want in Savannah, or anywhere else. Why should I care that you still love me?"

"That's all. Just that I love you."

Carolyn's face changed suddenly from rage to curiosity. "By the way how is your French whore?"

"I don't know. I haven't seen Yvette in a while. We are divorced now."

At that news Carolyn's eyes softened and the expression on her face relaxed. In the next instant, her demeanor again turned virulent.

"How convenient. And now you think you can come barging in here and I'll lie down on that very expensive carpet you're standing on and welcome you in my arms and yearn for the touch of your hands on my breasts that you used to love so much."

Matt was learning quickly the bile of a woman scorned. He stood up to leave.

"I'm sorry I ruined your day. I just wanted you to know I've never stopped loving you."

"Good day, Matt. You have yourself a good life."

He did not look back or indicate that he had heard. He walked quickly from the bank to his car. He started the engine and raced it several times in succession. Savagely engaging the transmission, he backed out of the parking slot with a squeal of tires. He stopped the car abruptly and sat staring out the windshield. He took a deep breath and relaxed his grip on the steering wheel. He sat a while longer, calming his shattered psyche.

Feeling himself more in control now, he switched on the radio at the instant the strangely haunting melody of *MacArthur Park* began playing. He felt drawn to the song about the breakup of a love affair. He listened intently to the lyrics.

*Someone left a cake out in the rain, I don't think that I can take it 'cause it took so long to bake it, I'll never have that recipe again.* Carolyn was gone for good. She would never again be his.

*I recall the yellow cotton dress, foaming like a wave on the ground around your knees.* He remembered the yellow dress, soft and simple, emphasizing her tiny waist. She loved to wear that dress in warm weather. He thought of the long springtime afternoons studying with her on the grass beneath the trees in the park, and the love they made when darkness offered an excuse to lay aside the books.

*After all the loves of my life, I'll be thinking of you and wondering why.* He did not have to wonder why. He knew why. It was greed and a desire for the life he had worked so hard for. Yvette could give him that and Carolyn could not. As he sat remembering days past, he smiled, thinking it ironic that she was wealthier now than he would ever be.

*There will be another song for me, and I will sing it. There will be another dream for me someone will bring it.* Of course there will be other loves.

*I will have the things that I desire and my passion flow like rivers from the sky.* The song ended and he smiled. "What the hell," he said aloud to the emptiness consuming him. "There's always Melody." Calmly, he drove from the bank parking lot and made his way toward Tybee. He would call her, and she would be eager and waiting.

On the island, he parked the car on Butler Avenue in front of his office. He tried to smile again as he took his place behind his desk. As hard as he tried, smiles would not come. The pain of Carolyn's rejection enveloped him like ocean mist in winter, penetrating the pores of his emotions to the core of his being, more painful than the anesthesia injection for a root canal he once had that brought tears to his eyes. He suddenly realized his eyes were moist now. He sat thinking how deeply he had loved her. Not only did she reject him, but he had never experienced contempt so deeply from anyone. He recalled the comfort and love he had felt in bed with her at Harvard on days exempt from classes.

He struggled to regain his composure and push Carolyn from his mind. Four or five minutes passed, and he began to feel better. He studied the telephone on his desk. Finally he picked it up, fondling it in his hand. He needed reassurance and relief from the pain he was feeling. He dialed Melody's number and listened. After six rings, he heard, "The person you have called...." The electronic voice finished the message, and Matt asked Melody to call him. He hung the phone on its cradle and fumbled through scraps of paper in a desk drawer till he found the one with Melody's cell number. He dialed it and again no answer. He left a message and waited. He knew she would call, and he would be waiting.

Matt busied himself with thumbing through the pages of the *Tybee Breeze* and other publications lying around the office. A little over two hours later, the phone rang. He lifted the receiver and, without checking the caller ID, answered with the usual hello.

"Matt?" The voice was familiar.

"Yes."

"Matt, I think I was a little too hard on you when you came by the bank this morning. I'm sorry."

Matt was relieved. "That's all right, Carolyn. I shouldn't have barged in like that without phoning first."

"I want you to know I'm ready to make it up to you. You will forgive me, won't you?"

"Of course I'll forgive you. What is your proposal?"

"Let me take you to dinner on Friday. My treat."

"Sounds great, but I will be happy to pick up the tab."

"No. I insist."

"Can't argue with a beautiful lady about a free meal. You're on."

They made the date and Matt hung up the phone. He busied away the afternoon and prepared to leave his office at a quarter to five. He opened the door and stepped one foot onto the sidewalk and the phone rang. He turned back and checked the caller ID. He hesitated. Should he answer it? The rings stopped and he listened to the message from the caller.

"Matt, we had a heart attack patient this afternoon. I just now got off work. I'm sorry I couldn't call you earlier. Call me on my cell."

The phone went silent, and Matt stood for a while wondering what to do. Maybe he should return Melody's call. Several seconds passed, and he jammed the key in the lock and twisted it. Without looking back he walked quickly to his car and drove to a restaurant in Tybee Oaks. He had been so miserable after his morning encounter with Carolyn that he had not even thought about lunch. Thinking about her now, he wondered which was greater, his hunger for food or for Carolyn.

On Friday night Matt drove to the gate of Carolyn's mansion and punched in the code she had given him. He drove through the gate and passed a large man seated on a golf cart. As Matt made his way to the mansion's door, the man in the golf cart followed and parked a hundred yards from the house. Matt rang the bell and an attractive, young black woman greeted him.

"Mrs. Winston will be with you in a moment. Would you like a drink? Sweet tea? Water? wine?"

"No thank you. I'm fine." The woman was not a typical maid. She was obviously well educated and probably well paid.

"Then have a seat and make yourself comfortable. You can turn on the TV if you like. Today's paper and magazines are on the table there. Help yourself. Mrs. Winston will be down momentarily." She flashed Matt a bright, confident, flirtatious smile and disappeared through an arched passageway.

Matt didn't look at his watch, but after what he calculated as about fifteen minutes, he began to feel a little anxious and impatient. He glanced around the room and focused a long time on the staircase on which he assumed Carolyn would descend. He entwined the fingers of both hands and stretched his arms in front of him. He glanced around the room again and picked up the TV remote. He punched it to life and turned to Anderson Cooper on CNN. He lost himself in the program, unaware of the passing time. During a commercial he checked his watch and realized he had been waiting an unusually long time. He switched off the TV and leaned back on the sofa and closed his eyes. After a short while, he fell into a light sleep. He awoke when he felt familiar lips softly touch his.

"I'm sorry I took so long to get dressed, but I knew you wouldn't mind. I promise you I'm worth waiting for."

Matt stole a quick look at his watch and thought for a brief moment that he did mind, but he said nothing. He had been waiting a little over an hour. Surely this was not her usual habit. No one could possibly believe it acceptable to be that rude and inconsiderate.

Over dinner on River Street at one of the several restaurants in warehouses used for storing cotton before that Georgia commodity went bust in the early 1950s, Matt and Carolyn talked about the times they had shared at Harvard and the years since they had last seen each other.

"I see that you aren't wearing a wedding ring. Is there a reason?" Matt had to have an answer to the question.

"Winston died three years ago. Massive heart attack."

*Winston? She called her dead husband Winston? That's cold.*

"We were in the process of a divorce when it happened. He was considerably older than I, and he had lost the enthusiasm and excitement of the early days of our marriage. I loved him at first, but I came to loathe the life I had with him. He left me with more money than I and my accountants can keep up with and a teenaged stepdaughter who is a royal pain in the ass. I can tolerate all of his money, but his daughter I could do without. To put it mildly, she's a bitch of the highest order."

Carolyn's criticism of her stepdaughter called to memory Matt's youth with an adult that did not like him. He lowered his head and stared at the top of the table and said nothing in reply.

The waiter brought the food. Carolyn cut into the steak and frowned. She glared at the young man serving the meal. *Probably a student,* Matt thought. "Do you see that red there? What did I ask for?"

"You asked for well done, ma'am."

"Does that look well done?"

"No ma'am."

"Then what does it look like?"

"It looks like not well done, ma'am."

"Take it! And when you bring it back, it had better be what I asked for."

"Yes ma'am. I'll do that." The waiter picked up the plate. It slipped from his fingers and fell back to the table with a loud *bonk!* He picked it up again, and when he turned toward the kitchen he stumbled and almost fell.

Carolyn sent the meal back several more times before finally accepting it. On the last serving, the waiter's hands were trembling and his face was flushed a deep pink when he set the food before her. Matt observed her behavior, thinking it incredible how much she had changed, how power seemed to have made her an entirely different person.

"And don't you dare leave that incompetent fool a tip, not a cent."

Matt looked at her briefly and then at his plate. He was no longer hungry. He placed his fork on the table, gripped together the fingers of his hands and propped his elbows on the table.

"Do you have to prop your elbows on the table, Matt? That is so pedestrian. Next thing, you'll be sucking on a toothpick like a damned Georgia hillbilly."

Matt removed his elbows from the table without responding verbally. After the meal he studied the check the waiter timidly placed on the table. He immediately handed the young man his credit card. Carolyn jerked it from his hand and placed her credit card and the check on the table. When it was returned, she signed it and wrote in the total with no tip.

Matt excused himself to the bathroom. Around a corner out of Carolyn's line of vision, he handed the waiter two twenty dollar bills. "You earned this, son." he said. He returned to Carolyn looking at her watch and glancing at the path he had taken when he had excused himself.

Leaving the restaurant Carolyn asked, "You didn't slip that little twerp a tip, did you?" Matt shook his head but said nothing.

After dinner the couple drove to Carolyn's place. Matt was happy to be back with the only woman he had ever loved as deeply as he loved Carolyn. He felt himself extremely lucky to be back in her bed, even though he was distracted and disconcerted somewhat by her constant directions and criticism of his lovemaking, often preceded or followed by tenderness.

One of the most devastating things a lover can do to a man is criticize him. The absolute worst, deal-breaking thing she can do is criticize his love making.

Matt's longing had been fulfilled, and he tolerated her behavior. *Things will get better. She's still angry because I dumped her. I will hang in and love her into the sweetness that she once was.*

After the loving, Matt sensed that Carolyn wanted him to leave and he did. He drove away mulling over in his mind Carolyn's behavior. *Maybe I ought to keep right on driving as far away as I can, as fast as I can, or else forget my way back to this address.*

But against his better judgment, Matt continued seeing Carolyn. He tried, but could not free himself from the obsession he felt for his first love. Time passed and he began to approach his time with her with trepidation instead of joyous anticipation.

He stopped calling her. And when she called, he sometimes either ignored the ringing phone or made excuses not to see her. He found himself more and more in the company of Melody, and he began to see in her something he had not recognized before.

# Twelve

January is usually the coolest month of winter on Tybee Island. But except for the first few days of the month, January 2012 did little to enhance the income of flannel shirt and overcoat merchants. Melody could remember only a handful of night-time temperatures that dropped to what she would think of as cold. Daytime temps ranged in the low 60s to the high 70s with the warmer days dominating the winter weather.

She did not like cold from any source, be it wind, rain, or ocean. In movies and on television, islands were always warm. It somehow seemed incongruous to her that an island could be anything but consistently warm, even though she grew up on Tybee and knew the feel of chilly winters.

She always dreaded late fall because winter would soon follow. But when late winter took its place among the tourists on the island fleeing their own frigid misery, her outlook brightened. The long, sunny days of spring could not be far behind. But she was grateful now that this winter had been mild.

The new year dawned on a Sunday. Melody tried to coax Matt into taking the annual Polar Plunge in the Atlantic. For a while he thought he might do it. But the first day of January started cold with a heavy fog, and at the last minute he declined. Melody, though, showed no fear and ran with more than eleven hundred other participants from different parts of the country and the world into the fifty-two degree surf. She dreaded the cold, but the Guinness Book of Records for the most people in swim caps was at stake, and she would do her part for her hometown. The attempt was successful and Tybee Island earned the honor.

In a few days the weather warmed, and Melody spent much of her free time walking alone on the beach. Occasionally, she had a pizza with Matt. She had not dated another man since meeting him. Suitors called, but she knew she would be bored and unengaged. Some invited her to accompany them to concerts at the Savannah Civic Center. She would have loved the Merle Haggard/Bob Dylan concert, but it wasn't worth the effort to try to be good company to dates in whom she had no interest.

The mild weather brought other good news. Hammers and building materials began a slow return to Tybee. Prior to the housing crash of 2008, the sounds of construction greeted almost every morning except Sundays. That sound had not been heard for some time now and Tybee, overall, had been in somewhat of a funk. Now, good times began a slow trek back, and the area began to experience some of the robustness of former days.

At first, Matt found the sounds annoying, but when he learned of their earlier demise and now their resurrection he rejoiced along with most other Tybee inhabitants. The darkest days of the past four years seemed to be at an end and some of the former vitality of the island appeared to be on the horizon.

While economic hope seemed to glow in the hearts of most residents, Matt did not see brightness at all in his personal life. He suffered long hours of doubt that his relationship with Carolyn would ever work out. Her behavior had him totally baffled. She could be the angel of old when she chose, but then her moods and attitude could quickly change when things did not go her way.

To try to find answers to the growing questions in his mind, Matt searched the volumes on relationships in the Tybee public library and on-line. The information he gathered seemed to point to borderline personality disorder, a condition most often manifesting itself in young women in early adulthood. Carolyn could be overly nurturing and agreeable at times, then quickly turn mean spirited. In those moods, she seemed to be thrashing out in dark malice intent on causing maximum pain to whatever victim crossed her. Sometimes it seemed that he was her favorite target. His university studies of psychology and sociology certainly would not qualify him to make that diagnosis, but if she were suffering from a condition of some kind, he could be more patient and understanding.

February came, and feeling bad about not joining Melody in the Polar Plunge, he agreed to participate in the Tybee Run Fest scheduled for the third and fourth of the month. He did not know if he could complete the twenty-six mile marathon, but for her he would try. The complete event was spread over two days in five separate races. The first leg of the contest was a 5K on Friday evening. Matt and Melody finished together at the reasonable time of thirty-eight minutes. And even though he had the advantage of longer legs, he had to struggle to keep up. His long days in the restrictive shadows of high-rise caverns in New York City had not prepared him for an active life on Tybee Island.

On Saturday morning, runners gathered for the seven o'clock start of the 10K. Matt received a call from Melody. She had been called to work to replace a colleague at home with a sick baby. Matt had been anticipating the day's events with her, and decided since she could not participate, he would forego the race. And since he was already dressed, he decided to hang around and watch the competition for a while. Milling about the starting line in the main parking lot on the south end, he turned when he felt a soft hand on his shoulder.

"How have you been? I haven't heard from you in a while. It's good to see you doing something healthy—if you can handle it."

Matt looked at the owner of the hand and forced a smile. "I've decided to sit this one out, Carolyn. It's good to see you," he lied.

"Oh. Can't take it, huh?" The condescension in her voice fell thicker than the early morning mist.

"Of course I can do it. I simply choose not to."

"Sure you can." Carolyn rolled her eyes. Her lips curled into a sarcastic smirk.

"If you want to see me run, I'll show you." Matt could not shrink from her contempt.

"Want to make a little side bet on who finishes first—or at all? Lunch maybe?" Carolyn's contempt intensified.

"You've got a bet. I'll take your free lunch." The sound of "free lunch" soured in Matt's mouth, but he said it before thinking.

The runners lined up and the race began. Matt sprang from the starting line and quickly advanced far out ahead of her—his first mistake. Carolyn paced herself behind him. Nearing the 5K mark, Matt's breath began to come fast without relieving the pleas from his lungs for more oxygen. The fire in the muscles of his legs screamed for relief.

Carolyn passed him and paced on down the course. Matt had by now figured out that he had started too fast. He watched Carolyn disappear around a corner and conceded that she would probably win the wager, but he would not stop even if his chest exploded or his legs erupted in flames on the finish line.

He rounded the corner and raised his focus from the ground. Up ahead Carolyn came into view. The next leg of the route was the beach run. Crossing the soft sand, Matt's stronger legs muscled him ahead of Carolyn. She watched him pass with a surprised look on her face. Matt went around her trying to hide the malice in his smile.

The race continued and Carolyn began to gain on him. Side-by-side they reached the Mile Run marker. Carolyn began to pull ahead. With every ounce of effort he could muster, Matt tried desperately to catch up to her. But no matter how he paced himself, pain wracked his legs and adequate breath would not come. He watched her cross the finish line six meters ahead of him.

She regained her breath and ability to speak first. "So, you made it, big man. I've got to hand it to you, with the stamina you've shown me in other areas, I didn't think you could do it."

Matt understood the innuendo and contempt of the statement. Anger that he was barely able to hold in check rose in his throat. He thought about walking away and leaving her standing in the parking lot with other runners looking on. But no matter how cruel she was and how angry he felt, he could not bring himself to humiliate her in that fashion.

"Maybe my stamina responds only to appropriate inspiration," he finally blurted, louder than he intended.

"You men always have the right answer, the right excuse, the right thing to say to excuse your flaws, don't you?"

"Maybe we do. Anyway, I owe you lunch."

At a restaurant with a taste of quiet elegance, a young woman dressed to match the ambiance of the facility led Matt and Carolyn to a table overlooking the ocean. The sea was at ebb tide, and the view seemed to calm their mutual animosity, and they enjoyed a pleasant lunch. They finished the meal and walked to the pavilion. Beach music from the sound system permeated the humid air. Time and pleasant surroundings healed much of their anger. Carolyn turned to look at Matt and dropped a closed fist on his leg.

"Matt, you are pulling away from me. Can you be honest and tell me where we stand?"

"It doesn't seem to be working for us, does it?"

"It could if you would listen to me and try. You haven't really given us a chance, have you?"

"I think I have. I can't figure out if you want me or not. Sometimes it seems you love me, then you don't."

"I do love you, Matt. But sometimes things don't go right, and I can't control my frustration and anger. If we had gotten married back then, things would be perfect with us. I know they would. We would be living in the Hamptons with two kids and a dog, and I wouldn't need to work. You would provide well for us, and I would be there to greet the children when they came home from school and you from work."

The sentimental picture that Carolyn painted recalled in Matt the dreams they had talked about before he met and married Yvette. He thought of how he had anticipated sharing a family with Carolyn as his wife. That was a dream he had never fully purged from his mind and his heart. Even now he struggled to let it go. Somewhere in his heart he still longed to see the emergence of a Carolyn of another time and place, nearly perfect in mind, body, and spirit.

The afternoon wore on and the lovers began to enjoy their time together. Near five o'clock Carolyn asked Matt to come home with her. "I would really like that. Besides, you have some things there you need to pick up since it seems you won't be coming around much anymore."

"Did I say I'm not coming around anymore?"

"Action speaks louder than words I'm told."

"I've been busy." Matt could not bring himself to let her go, even though he knew in his heart that he should. "I'll go with you."

Melody would be coming home any minute now, and for reasons he could not explain to himself, he did not want her to see him with Carolyn. He and Melody were friends and nothing more. Why should he care if she saw him with Carolyn?

Matt followed Carolyn's Town Car in his Mercedes. He didn't know what to expect when they reached her estate, so he went prepared for hurt or heaven. He did not particularly care to make love to her, but if she initiated romance he would not reject her advances.

The next day was Sunday, and she would not have to work. She would have no reason to put him out when she finished with him, even though she had nothing pressing to do the next day. But he could not depend on her to take him back to the island. Besides, she may invite him in, and change her mind if things did not go her way.

At her home, Carolyn not only invited him to come in, but insisted on it. Luckily, the night progressed smoothly. But after a long session of love-making, she sent Matt on his way. For the first time ever he protested, reminding her that the next day was Sunday.

"You come into my home and enjoy my hospitality and take the love I freely offer. After that you go away." Carolyn seemed to be restraining an expression of resentment. Apparently, she still had not forgiven him for dumping her. "Those are the rules, buster," she stated with authority and finality.

Matt felt like a prostitute—or worse, a bondservant. She had used him and now wanted him out of her way. "When do I get to make some rules?" He shot back. He wondered how long he could hold out hope for a change and tolerate Carolyn's abuse.

"Don't count on it, buster. Good night."

She closed the door and Matt walked away. He was not angry, nor was he disappointed. He was numb, absent emotion. The time had come for him to have some say in a relationship that should be a fifty-fifty proposition or something close to that. But deep in his heart, he knew that with Carolyn that would never be. But he would work harder at trying to please her and give their relationship one more chance.

For the next several weeks, Matt spent as much time with Carolyn as he could. They watched the Irish Heritage parade held annually on Tybee prior to the big Saint Patrick's Day parade in Savannah. The Tybee event began at 3 p.m., long after the banks had executed their Saturday early closings. Carolyn cared little for the parade, but she had customers from the island. She figured it wouldn't hurt to go, except for the wasted time. Going with Matt would ease some of the pain of watching all the spectators pretend to be Irish, and the childish antics of the Shriners, and the endless screech of bagpipes.

Melody would want to be at the Tybee parade and Matt was relieved that she had duty at the hospital that Saturday, but he had not counted on her rushing back to the island when her shift ended at 3 p.m. He did not want her to see him with Carolyn. In his heart he did know why, but he was not ready to let it happen. The heart loves who it will, and Carolyn had a hold on his that he could not shake loose—at least not now.

They were standing on the corner of 15th and Butler when Melody walked up to him.

"Hi. I was hoping I'd find you here on the south end." She placed her hand on Matt's arm. The over-sized smile on her face faded when he pulled away from her. Carolyn straightened and glared at the girl. A strange expression covered Matt's face. Melody did not understand his cold response. He finally regained his composure and introduced the two women. Both wondered at his behavior. They soon realized that something more than casual acquaintance existed between each of them and Matt.

He had no ties to Melody. He owed her nothing—maybe. He was not sure. At the present he had neither ties nor obligations to Carolyn either. He felt awkward, guilty, and confused. Melody was simply herself, kind and gentle and easy to be with; Carolyn was self-centered, demanding, and would have everything she wanted—including other men if she chose to. She was definitely not the woman he had shared his life with at Harvard. Had money changed her that much? Or was it the world that had made her what she was? Perhaps she was punishing him for dumping her for "the rich French whore." Maybe his rejection of her had soured her on him, and all men. She seemed bitter against everyone, never really happy or enjoying their activities together, her attitude and behavior constantly encroaching on his own joy. But something in the depths of his soul chained him to her, and he could not let her go again. Despite her abusive behavior toward him—and others—he clung to the hope that he could love her into being the woman he had cared for so deeply in another time. Somewhere inside him that love still lingered like the sweet taste of chocolate after it has been swallowed. Despite lingering doubts about their future together, he had continued his relationship with Carolyn, anticipating the emergence of the woman he had loved so deeply in another day.

Melody soon recognized the awkwardness of the situation and excused herself. "Well," she said to Matt without looking at him, "I just wanted to say hello." She glanced at Carolyn. "Nice to meet you. Y'all have a nice time. My friends are missing me." She retreated quickly into the crowd. A few steps out, she turned to look at Matt watching her walk away. He saw the moisture in her eyes. Hurt and shame flooded his heart.

"Who was that little hussy?" Carolyn looked at Matt with rage in her eyes. "Don't lie to me. I know something is going on with you two. That was obvious."

Matt stiffened. "She's not a hussy. She's a friend. That's all. Just a friend that I run into every now and then. She lives on the island."

"You make sure a friend is all she is. I want you to stay away from her," Carolyn demanded.

"So, If I meet her coming down Tybrisa Street, I cross to the other side?"

"If that's what it takes to avoid her, yes. Cross the damn street."

"You expect me to avoid a friend while you carry on with Lord knows who?"

"Yes I do. All of that is in the past now. I want it to be me and you from now on. Our love was strong once. It can be again and that's what I want." Carolyn pointed a finger at Matt and gave him a hard look. It's me and you from now on. You've done your thing, I've done mine. That's all in the past now." She paused and moved closer to Matt asserting herself more aggressively. "And if I ever catch you with that slut, she'll be sorry, and you'll be sorrier."

Matt stiffened and his face turned a deep red. "Please don't call her that name. She is a decent girl, one of the most decent I know." He didn't want to start world war three, but he had to defend Melody.

"Why are you defending her? Are you saying she's more decent than me?"

"I was not comparing. I simply stated the fact that she is a decent girl."

Carolyn stomped away. Matt watched her go and did not try to stop her.

# Thirteen

$\mathcal{A}$fter missing her for several days, Matt decided that maybe Carolyn was right. Maybe he had been seeing too much of Melody and needed to spend more time with her. She seemed ready now to reconnect with him. He began thinking marriage, and if she was going to be his wife, he would have to accept her as she was. Sure, she was wound a little too tight, and maybe her temper stayed spring-loaded in the cocked position. Sure, she could be feisty and unreasonable at times, and she could be contemptuous, but the good times trumped the bad. Usually the difficult times did not last long. She would conquer her rage and things would be beautiful again—even though her recent tantrums seemed to be lasting longer.

Matt stopped attending Sunday services and lunch with Florence and her guests, and he hardly ever saw the philosopher and Robert. He included the two men once at a Sunday lunch with Carolyn at a downtown restaurant, and she demanded that he never invite "those disgusting people" to anything she was involved in again. Matt missed his old friends, but not enough to tear himself away from time with Carolyn.

The heart goes where it will, and the mystery of why abuse is sometimes tolerated in a romance will never be solved. Reports of gone-too-far abuse pour daily from TV and other media. But a more perplexing mystery, perhaps, is why would someone deliberately heap pain onto a loved one?

Nevertheless, Matt continued to love Carolyn despite her contemptuous and tasteless behavior. But after a while, he missed his old friends and found himself allowing Melody to flow gently into his thoughts. At these times a feeling of warmth and comfort that had begun slipping away settled over him.

Late on a Sunday night in March, Matt returned home from a day with Carolyn. The phone rang as he entered the living room of his condo. He looked at the caller ID and recognized Melody's number. He held the phone at arm's length and let it ring until it went silent. He began to undress for a shower. Thinking of Melody's call, an uneasy feeling gnawed at him. The feeling would not go away, would not let him go. After the shower he sat on the side of his bed and dialed Melody's number.

"I missed your call. What's up?"

"It's John Wayne. I thought you might want to know he was admitted to the hospital early this afternoon."

"What happened?"

"He collapsed on River Street. Robert had the presence of mind to call 9-1-1. He's really torn up about this. The doctors don't know what's wrong with John. We're doing some tests. I'll let you know as soon as I hear something."

"Tell John I'll see him in the morning."

"I will. But don't come too soon. We'll be busiest with him early."

"Tell him I'll be there a little before noon. And, Melody, thanks for calling. It's good to hear from you."

"That's surprising. I quit calling when you stopped answering my calls."

"I'm sorry. That won't happen again. Let me know if anything changes with John."

"You have a good one, Matt."

He heard a click followed by a low hum. Leaving the line open, he sat staring at the phone for several minutes remembering Melody, remembering the warmness, softness, and fragrance of her, the taste of her kisses. He pushed the off button of the phone and lay on the bed. Concern for John, and thoughts of Melody filled his mind. Eventually he dozed, but he did not sleep soundly. Conscious thoughts through the night were filled first with John then with Melody. Feelings of guilt pervaded his sleeplessness. He had virtually deserted two good, caring friends, and now one was ill and needed him, the other, forever strong and whole that he needed. He had to do something to make things right. By all means he would see what he could do to help the philosopher. That would be the first order of business in the morning.

The restless night finally ended, and morning came. Matt dressed and went to a light breakfast at a restaurant on Butler Avenue. Afterwards, he went to his office for a while to give John's doctors time to do their work.

He checked the *Tybee Breeze* to see if there was something he may have missed. Finding nothing new, he thumbed through the *Savannah Morning News*. At about ten o'clock, he drove to the hospital and found John in bed in his room. Robert sat in a chair near the bed, concern clouding his face, lack of sleep clearly visible.

"I don't know what's wrong with me, barrister. The doctors don't either yet. I've been feeling something for some time now. I've been unusually tired and weak. I'm nauseous a lot. Don't want to eat. And when I do, more often than not, it comes back up. I feel really bad, barrister."

"The doctors will get you fixed up and you'll be out of here in no time. I'm sure of it."

"I wish I was as certain as you, barrister. But one thing is for sure, I'm going to get out of here soon. They're treating me well, and I'm confident of their skills. But I can't stay here. Do you realize I'm sleeping in a clean bed with clean sheets and everything?" John paused and chuckled. His present care compared to the years under the bridge seemed ironic and amusing. Matt and Robert showed no evidence of agreement.

"Anyway, I've got to get out of here. This is not me. Besides, I don't want the money that is going to the mission for my friends spent to keep me in luxury. I have Medicare, of course. Not that I've ever used it. Never felt I needed to. All those shots and examinations are just fluff. Medicare won't pay all the bills anyway, and I don't want them spending their limited funds on me."

"That's foolish, John. You need medical attention. If you can't handle the expenses, I'll see that they get paid. You need to concentrate on getting well."

"I don't want to sound pessimistic, barrister, but no matter how much money is spent, I don't think I'm going to make it."

"Sure you are," Matt responded quickly. Robert swallowed hard.

Matt left the two men at the hospital, hoping the next news from John would be good. He returned to the island and sat on his deck listening to the music coming from the pavilion and watching activities on the beach. The March weather was still a little cool for Georgia natives, but the spring breakers, who had started arriving from northern, western, and even Southern colleges and universities, seemed comfortable enough in their shorts and bikinis. He watched the joy unfolding on the beach contrasting with the sadness in his heart for John and the people who loved the philosopher.

After an hour or two, the warm sun and cool breezes lulled Matt into a light sleep. When he awoke, the sun was on its way down behind Tybee River and Little Tybee Island. He opened his eyes, yawned, and stretched. He thought about calling Melody to see if she had news of John's condition. He lifted the phone, but before he could dial, it began ringing. He punched it on and it was silent for several seconds. He thought he heard a sob and Melody's voice. When she finally spoke, Matt could tell she was softly crying.

"It's cancer, Matt."

"Are you sure? Sometimes doctors make mistakes. Can we get a second opinion?"

"Matt, we don't make mistakes about cancer. The oncologists think it started in his prostate, but it has metastasized. It's all over him now. There's not much we can do but try to make his passing as painless and comfortable as possible."

The phone went silent for several seconds, maybe even a minute. Matt sat processing news that he did not want to accept.

Melody seemed to understand and said nothing, waiting until he was ready to listen again, ready to speak.

"We've got to do something," he said finally.

"Matt, you've got to understand, there's nothing we can do." The phone went silent again.

"There's got to be something we can do."

"We can do everything possible to make it easier for him. That's all we can do." Melody was the health professional now in control. "I spoke with his doctors. They agreed to let you tell him and Robert. I'll go with you. I'm on duty until seven this evening. If you can come on in, we can speak with him when you get here."

"Sure. I'll be right there. Give me thirty."

"See you when you get here."

In a few minutes, Matt was on his way to the hospital in Savannah. When he got there, Melody was waiting for him. She gave him a weak smile, but neither spoke. They knew what the other was feeling. Speaking was unnecessary. They would save their words for John and pray that they could manage something comforting. They walked into his room. John looked at them and read their faces. They moved slowly and silently to his side and looked down at him. Matt looked at Robert and read the pain in his eyes.

John could stand the silence no longer. Someone had to say something. It appeared that it would have to be him.

"It's cancer, isn't it?"

"Yes." The word eased from Matt's mouth in little more than a whisper. Robert rose to his feet. "No! It can't be."

"I'm afraid it can, Robert. It is." Melody spoke softly but in a direct, professional tone. Robert sat back down and buried his face in his big hands. Matt and Melody could tell that this large man, who could weather all the hardships that life had thrown at him, was sobbing softly.

John could stand the drama no longer. "Listen, guys. It seems my race is about over. I can accept that. My life has been an uphill struggle—mostly against myself and my own demons. The world has been better to me than I've been to myself. I

93

acknowledge that." John paused and took several deep breaths as if struggling with oxygen depletion.

He shifted his weight on the bed and spoke again.

"But after all is said and done, my life has been an adventure, and I look forward to the discoveries of the next."

"We'll pray," Robert broke in. "Matt can get that church he attends to pray. We can beat this."

"No, my friend, I don't want anyone praying for me. I can do my own praying. Prayer is personal. Others can pray for you, your clergy can pray for you. But the heart of prayer must come from within, prayed with earnestness and faith that the prayer will be answered." John looked at the ceiling and repositioned his body on the bed. Heavy silence filled the room. When he had made himself comfortable, he resumed speaking.

"Miracles sometimes happen, but they are not driven by individuals such as faith healers or television evangelists. Prayer for the alteration of natural physics is unreasonable, but sometimes unusual things happen and no one knows why or how. But all-in-all, perhaps it is better to pray for courage, strength, and faith to deal with the unfortunate whims of fate." John paused and looked at Robert and patted his arm. Then he turned to Melody and Matt.

"Don't pray for me or ask your church to pray. I don't know what waits on the other side, but I have my faith, and whatever befalls me I know I'll be all right. I have to rely on one of the greatest philosophies ever written. I believe it was the author of the Book of Hebrews that wrote: 'Faith is seeing what's beyond sight/ Believing what's beyond reason/Receiving what's beyond comprehension. Now faith is the substance of things hoped for, the evidence of things not seen.'" John paused again. He seemed to be tiring, but he was not quite through yet.

"Down through the ages, men have speculated about the afterlife, but no one really knows for sure. Who has been a witness? Plato, for example, one of the great philosophers of ancient days, concluded that the soul exists before birth and survives death of the body, and our life on earth is only a shadow of what is to come in the reality of the hereafter where we really begin to live. I've met all my demons—I think. There may be one or two floating around in obscure regions of the old psyche. But at least I have confronted the major devils and come to terms with them. Conquered? Perhaps not. But I have made peace with them, and that is liberating to the soul. And this I know: my life has been an adventure, and I look forward to the discoveries of the next. And whatever befalls me will be good. Wherever they are, I'll be with my parents, and Anna, and Angelica, and all my friends like y'all. Yes, I will eventually be with all of you again." He grew silent, blinked at the ceiling then turned to look into Matt's eyes. "That's a good word, barrister. 'Y'all. As Southern as it gets."

John repositioned himself again and rested. He looked around the room at the faces before him. "I have a confession that I must acknowledge while I can. In the grand scheme of things, I know I have failed miserably in this life. I have believed for a long time that the best use of life is to contribute to something that lasts longer than we do, and I've failed." He paused and looked at Matt. "And you, barrister, I want to leave you with some unsolicited advice. I've thought about this for a long time, and I'm going to do it. I'm going to leave you with a quote from Thomas Wolfe's *You Can't Go Home Again*. 'I think the enemy is here before us with a thousand faces, but I think that all his faces wear one mask. I think the enemy is single selfishness and compulsive greed.'"

Matt did not respond. He would not object nor deny that maybe he had been selfish and overly ambitious most of his life. But the philosopher's "unsolicited advice" troubled him, and he would think on it some more. The only thing he could think of now was that while money may not buy happiness, it certainly could stave off a lot of misery.

John continued talking about the philosophies of life after death until in midsentence sleep overtook him. Melody pulled the covers around him, and she and Matt left him alone with Robert, who opened his eyes briefly and raised a hand in a limp gesture of goodbye. The last thing they saw before closing the door was John sleeping and Robert sitting with his head in his hands.

Walking down the hallway, Melody suddenly stopped. The professional caregiver had slipped from her grasp. She was now a caring friend grieving the loss of a loved one. She left Matt alone in the hallway and stepped into a restroom. She did not turn on the light. Alone in the darkness, she wept. When she finally emerged from her hide-away, she was Nurse Melody, professional health-care worker fully in control.

For several nights after that terrible event, Matt lay awake troubled. Wakeful through the long nights, he pondered the direction of his life, the pursuit of wealth, and love, and family. He loved Carolyn with all his heart, but he knew he would never be happy with her. Melody, on the other hand was easy as a cool summer breeze. And his friend John would soon be gone. Everything seemed so complicated. Why couldn't people live healthy and happy lives? It just didn't make much sense. It seemed to him that life offered choices. The right choices lead to happiness; wrong choices lead to sorrow. Should he answer Carolyn's phone calls? She called often, and left angry messages on his answering machine demanding that he return her calls. Those he ignored also.

On a night when his eyes had become scratchy from loss of sleep, his mind wandered to Melody and the Mardi Gras Tybee event they attended the first week of March. She had arranged her schedule so that she could participate in all the activities. Matt, of course, joined her. She was a good buddy, a fun companion.

They watched the parade and attended the masquerade ball and street party on Tybrisa, and danced to the music of two amazing bands. Both Matt and Melody were decked out in costume, Melody complete with a stick mask emphasizing her eyes and lips. Before the night was over, Matt found himself mesmerized by the sparkling beauty of her blue eyes and the sensuousness of her full lips. The vision filled him with an urge to kiss her. She would welcome that. But she would expect more, a promise he was not yet ready to fulfill.

When the band had played the last song of the night, Matt walked Melody to her apartment. At her door she paused before inserting the key. She lowered the mask from her eyes and turned to face Matt. "Well, it's been fun," she said looking into his eyes. He returned her gaze and they stood in place for a long time. When Matt made no move, she raised herself on her toes and kissed him lightly on the lips and turned quickly and disappeared behind the closed door. Matt stood looking at the door. He savored the tender kiss and wished something would move her to burst through the door and fly into his arms. He would hold her body close to his and devour the sensual sweetness of her lips.

Now in this early morning in mid-March, he closed his eyes and finally drifted into a light sleep. Dreams of Melody came upon him, and when he again awoke, disappointment enveloped him.

He did not want to wake up.

# Fourteen

The 17th of March was quickly approaching, and Savannah—fourth largest city in Georgia—was preparing for one of the most elaborate Saint Patrick's Day parades in the world.

New York City's event follows a one and a half mile route through Manhattan; Boston, home of the first known St. Patrick's Day Parade held in 1737, winds through the Irish neighborhood on the South Side for almost two hours; the Savannah parade makes its way through two and a half miles of downtown streets for four hours. All activities surrounding the event anticipated since last year's parade was being made ready. *Going Places* magazine estimated that almost a million individuals, and visitors in groups from around the nation and the world, sometimes witnessed or participated in the festivities.

On the day of the parade, John was still in the hospital. Matt went by to see him before picking up Carolyn to connect with the CAT bus downtown. She had prevailed on him so hard to take her, he eventually gave in. He wondered why she would attend an event that she obviously would not enjoy. Melody traded shifts with another nurse so that she could attend the parade with Matt. That plan was squashed, however, when Carolyn insisted that he accompany her to the big parade. Matt had finally told Melody about his relationship with Carolyn and how they had been together for a long time, and that he was hoping to rekindle a romance with her. Melody accepted the unpleasant information with tears in her eyes, but did not protest.

The Savannah parade, as always, was well planned and began right on time. Matt and Carolyn were in position on Bay Street. They had found a comfortable shaded spot in anticipation of the four-hour parade. Bands from high schools, colleges; and local, national, and international institutions marched and played their way along the parade route. The Shriner's go-carts and Hillbillies delighted children and adults alike.

"They are so ridiculous," Carolyn declared. "If this thing weren't such a big deal here, I wouldn't participate at all. Sometimes you just have to play the game. It's such a waste of time for so many businesses and schools to close to prepare for this foolishness."

The uneasy feeling that Matt had begun sensing for some time now in Carolyn's presence fell upon him again like a Massachusetts blizzard, even though the Savannah temperature had warmed to a comfortable seventy-five degrees.

Matt lost himself in the parade, especially delighted to see up close for the first time ever the Budweiser Clydesdales. He felt a little nostalgic when the New York firemen and policemen marched by. He ran out to shake the hands of some firemen, and recognizing some of the police officers with whom he had become acquainted in court appearances, he followed them down the street in animated conversation. When he finally returned to Carolyn, he was greeted by cold eyes and a stern expression. "Why did you come back? You could join the damn parade and spend the rest of the day with it and your buddies. I can do very well on my own."

"I'm sorry. I got caught up in the excitement of seeing someone from home. I got carried away. I'm sorry."

"I'm tired of this foolishness anyway. Let's go down to River Street and get some lunch and a drink. And if you leave me again, you can keep on going."

"I said I'm sorry. What else do you want from me?" Matt snapped.

Carolyn looked at him with an expression of surprise, shocked at the irritation and boldness in his voice, but she made no reply.

On River Street the revelers inched elbow to elbow along the ballast stones. The crowds and the carefree atmosphere reminded Matt of Mardi Gras in New Orleans—except that here people were more civil, and the area was cleaner and no one urinated on the street or displayed their breasts—at least not in public. By the time the couple reached the restaurant that Carolyn chose, tables and bar tools were full. Visitors to Savannah for the event formed long waiting lines outside businesses up and down the street. Carolyn assessed the situation and suggested that they go to her place.

"My domestic staff if off today for all of this foolishness, but I can cook, and I have a full, well stocked bar. We can have a sandwich and I'll fix dinner later."

"I hate to leave the festivities here. There's so much excitement in the air. But that sounds great. And you can cook?"

"Of course I can cook. With my money I can do anything, but the good part is I don't have to. I do what I want to, when I want to. Today I want to prepare a dinner for you." Carolyn looked up at Matt. He returned the look, and she turned her face to his and kissed him softly on the lips.

*Why can't she be this sweet all the time? How long can moments like this keep me coming back?*

They slowly made their way through the crowds and caught the CAT bus to Oglethorpe Mall where Matt's Mercedes was parked. They drove to Carolyn's home and had sandwiches on the deck by her Olympic-sized swimming pool. Matt preferred beer, but at Carolyn's insistence, they sipped chilled wine for a couple of hours. At a few minutes past five, Carolyn went into the kitchen to begin preparing dinner. Matt sat alone on the deck. Looking at the water in the swimming pool, he thought of the view from the deck of his condo. He listened to the roar of the pool's circulation pump contrasting with his memory of gentle waves falling on the Tybee shore at ebb tide, and the awesome crash of the surf at high sea. He remembered the especially high tides of winter. Listening easy on still winter evenings, he had often heard the mesmerizing sounds of the surf from almost every point on the island. Thinking about that now, he imagined that if the voice of God were ever heard, that is how it would sound, strong yet soothing as a whisper on a warm, soft wind. Carolyn's estate was impressive, but the beach and his friends there felt more like home.

After a dinner of New York strip steak with all the trimmings, Matt helped Carolyn empty the dishes and load the dishwasher. "I've done enough domestic stuff for today. Mona can wash the dishes tomorrow. Let's have another glass of wine, watch a couple of reruns on TV, and retire to the bedroom for real entertainment."

"That's the best idea I've heard all day."

In bed shortly thereafter, Matt was pleased that Carolyn was more tender, more considerate, more like the old days than any time since they had reconnected. *Maybe we can make this work after all.*

Following the extended loving, Carolyn lay on Matt's shoulder with his left arm around her. They lay quietly enjoying the afterglow. After a long while, Carolyn patted his chest and said, "OK, big guy. I'm tempted to let you stay the night, but I'm going to reluctantly send you on your way."

"Aw, man. Do you have to? I'm ready for a good night's sleep with heaven in my arms."

"Beautiful words, big man, but you know the rules."

"All right, if you insist. But you are going to miss the best night of cuddling you've ever dreamed of."

"Perhaps so, but I do insist."

Matt kissed her lightly and rolled out of bed. Carolyn got up and wrapped herself in a robe. "Get dressed and I'll walk you out."

Matt left the bedroom thinking Carolyn's rule peculiar, *but of course, she wouldn't send me out if we were married. This thing could work out. I think I'll start shopping for a ring.*

They walked to the living room with Matt's arm around Carolyn's waist. At the front door they embraced. Matt moved to kiss Carolyn and the door flew open. A young woman burst through the door on unsteady legs. Carolyn pushed away from Matt and glared at the girl.

"Do you know what time it is, young lady?" Carolyn demanded. "Where have you been until two o'clock in the morning?"

"I've been celebrating Saint Patrick, Patron Saint of Ireland." The girl waved a finger in the air, weaved, and almost fell. "He wasn't Irish, wasn't Roman Catholic, wasn't born on March 17th, and did not drive snakes out of Ireland, but I celebrated him anyway."

"You're drunk. Who gave you liquor? Or a better question is, what did you do for liquor?" Carolyn paused and looked at Matt. "This is Hannah, the stepdaughter I told you about."

Matt extended his hand. "Happy to meet you, Hannah." He shook her hand and smiled at recognizing her. He took a step backwards and looked at the girl. "My, you are beautiful, beautiful as a, a what? a princess?"

"I see that grin on your face, buster. If you dare to run your mouth or make jokes about hard-hearted Hannah from Savannah I'll neuter you right here in my dear mother's house, the house my father gave to my dear mother." Hannah turned a cold, sarcastic gaze to Carolyn.

"You see what I told you, Matt. A bitch of the highest order. Shows no respect to anyone."

"Maybe I am a bitch, but I'm an honest bitch, unlike the other bitch in this room."

Carolyn took Hannah's shoulders in her hands and shook her hard. The girl almost lost her balance. "If you weren't your dead father's daughter, I would beat hell out of you right here and teach you some respect." Carolyn released Hannah's shoulders and turned to walk away.

"If you would give me some of my father's money, I would be out of here and you wouldn't be bothered with me again."

Carolyn walked back to face her stepdaughter. "You will be eighteen in a few months and you will have some of your father's money that I can no longer control. My responsibility for you will end in accordance with his orders. Then you can go straight to hell for all I care.'

"And you, Mother Dearest, can go fuck yourself."

In a single instant, Carolyn's eyes caught fire. Her face twisted into a pale, menacing mask. "Don't you ever use that disgusting word in my presence again. I hear it in the streets, in the clubs, and in the restaurants. I don't have to tolerate it in my own home." Her right hand shot out lightning fast, striking Hannah hard across the face. The blow turned her half way around. She stumbled, almost fell then regained her balance. She turned to face her stepmother. Matt prepared to step between the two women. Hannah glared at Carolyn, years of pent-up resentment flashing in her eyes.

"You never loved my father. Everyone knew that. He knew that. Oh, yes. You loved the lure of his money at first. But when you got the money, it became more important than he was. At that point he was just an old man, an old man with moles on his back, and more hair in his ears than on his head, and spider veins around his ankles, and an inability to get it up. I know that. Do you know how I know that? He told me. He told me that's what you said to him. You said all those terrible things to him. He cried when he shared with me the cruelty in the way you treated him. He cried and you killed him. Yes, his heart was bad, but you squeezed the last drop of life from it, and he gave up. He could not make you love him the way he needed you to love him, and it killed him." Hannah's body heaved in uncontrollable sobs. Carolyn glared silently at her stepdaughter with unrestrained, undeniable rage flashing in her eyes.

Hannah gained control and stood upright. She seemed stone cold sober now. "And you have the audacity to call me a bitch. Who's the bitch now, Mother Dearest?"

Carolyn screamed at her. "Get out. Get out of my house now and don't come back. I'll have Mona and Reginald pack and deliver your things wherever you are. And don't expect money from me or your father's estate until the allotted time. You can get by the best way you can."

"I will go gladly, and I hope to never cross paths with you again." Hannah walked through the door and closed it gently behind her. She was calm now and at peace. A long, pervasive issue in her life was resolved. She would live in her car for a while or maybe move in with one of her boyfriends. When she received her inheritance, she would find a place of her own, maybe even a home on Tybee. She could afford to live wherever she wanted then.

Matt had seen some of the toughest characters imaginable, and some of the fiercest confrontations possible protecting the fortunes of some of the largest corporations in the world, but the incident he had witnessed tonight in this family left him shaken.

"You're terribly upset, Carolyn. I'm sure you need time to sort this out. I'll call you tomorrow." Matt kissed her lightly. Her lips were hard and cold. He walked quickly away.

He started his car and drove slowly along the driveway. Near the gate he slowed to a stop behind Hannah sitting in her Mustang. He sat for a while then stepped out of the car. He walked to her driver-side window. She saw him and pushed the down button.

"What's up? You got car trouble?"

"No."

"Is there anything I can help you with?"

Hannah wiped her eyes with a small white tissue and looked at Matt. "I'm a little upset, but I'll be OK." She sniffed and touched the tissue to her nose.

"Where are you staying tonight?"

"I don't know. I don't have any money, so I guess I'll crash right here. It's not long till morning anyway."

"You don't need to do that. It wouldn't look right for you to stay at my place tonight, but I can put you up in a hotel." Another thought came to Matt's mind. "Or, I have a friend who would be delighted to have your company."

"No thanks. I've dealt with enough jerks tonight. You're going to have to find someone else for him."

"Oh, no. It's nothing like that. I know a sweet old lady that would be glad to have you."

"I wouldn't want to impose on anyone."

"It would not be an imposition. My friend Florence would love you."

"It would be nice to take a shower in the morning. You sure I wouldn't be in her way?"

"Positive. Follow me to Tybee." Matt turned to go to his car. Hannah called out to him.

"Matt." He stopped and turned to face her. "I'm sorry I acted the way I did in your office that day last summer. I don't know what I was thinking. I apologize also for stalking you."

"That's OK, kid. My mother used to say 'children will be children.'"

"Just wait, buddy. A few more months and you won't be able to say that to me again." Hannah smiled. She was feeling better now.

"Follow me. I'll drive slowly in case you are still feeling the hootch."

The couple reached Tybee, and Matt rang Florence's doorbell. They listened to the rustling of sleepy movement and agitated mumbling coming from inside the house. Finally, Florence opened the door.

"What the hell are you doing ringing my doorbell at this time of the night, sonny?" Florence peered at them in the dim light. "And who is that gorgeous creature with you? Don't you dare tell me you've been up to monkey business with that child. Come on in, and you'd better have a damn good story, waking God-fearing Christian ladies in the middle of the friggin night with a baby on your arm. You'd better have a damn good one, sonny!"

Matt and Hannah followed Florence to the living room. Hannah looked scared and unsure. With her hands folded tightly in front of her, she listened as Matt explained her situation to Florence. When he finished the explanation, Florence's face brightened. She was fully awake now. "Well hell fire, of course you can stay here, honey. You can stay as long as you like, if you can tolerate my humble offerings.

"Yes, ma'am. Your house is beautiful. Thank you for your kindness, and I will repay you. Matt didn't tell you this, but I'll be a millionaire in a few months."

"Yeah. And I'll be Mary Kay Andrews."

"No, ma'am. Really."

Matt smiled and said nothing to confirm Hannah's statement. Florence stood up and looked at the girl. "Come on, honey. I'll show you to your room. You have a bathroom right outside your door." They reached the elevator and Florence pushed the button. When the elevator door opened, Florence turned to Matt and said, "Go home and go to bed, sonny. You look like warmed-over death sucking on a friggin soda cracker. And lock my damn door on your way out."

"Good night, ladies." Matt did as Florence demanded. He went home and fell into bed. This had been a long, trying day.

But not as trying as would be wrought by the state of affairs Carolyn would unload on him much too early on Monday morning.

# Fifteen

$\mathcal{M}$att planned to sleep in on Monday morning, but at a little before nine his phone rang. "Matt, I need a lawyer." It was Carolyn.

"You are a lawyer."

"Not really, Matt. I've never had a license or practiced in Georgia. It's not a big thing. Some stupid kid on a bicycle ran in front of me."

"How bad was he hurt?"

"Just scratched up a little. Destroyed his bike. He jumped off the thing before he ran into me. They took him to the hospital, but I think they'll send him on to school. Oh, Matt, you must know how upset I was the other night. I haven't slept a wink all weekend."

"I guess we're all a little short on sleep today. I'll be there around lunchtime. We'll talk about it then." Matt was not ready to see Carolyn. He wondered if he would ever want to see her again. He began turning over in his mind scenarios for breaking up with her. For him the relationship had been strained since the beginning of their reconciliation. Carolyn was the opposite of the girl he had loved in college. He was accepting behavior that he should not. Maybe he didn't love her as much as he thought he did. Maybe he no longer loved her at all.

Matt punched the "end" button on his phone and pulled the covers up to his neck. After a half hour or so without falling asleep again he rolled out of bed and took a shower. He took his time dressing and strolled to a restaurant on Butler. After three cups of coffee, he went to his office and scanned the morning papers. Finding no news of particular interest, he called Florence to see if Hannah made it to school.

"The child was up before me. That's a sharp little kid you dragged in here, sonny. Reminds me of Brenda Lynne."

"Who is Brenda Lynne?"

"Oh, I've never told you about Brenda Lynne?"

"No, you haven't."

"Oh, she was the sweetest child ever. Beautiful and sweet. I'll tell you about her sometime."

Matt did not question Florence further, but he sensed in her voice something that told him Brenda Lynne was someone special. He would not let her forget her promise to tell him more.

Carolyn was waiting when Matt arrived at the seafood restaurant on Montgomery Crossroads. He could tell she was irritated because she had to wait a few minutes for him, but she said nothing to confirm the obvious. Deep in his heart, he took quiet joy at keeping her waiting and her irritation.

They entered the restaurant and placed their order. "Matt, you know I have the money to pay the little twerp if something comes up, but I don't want to. And I don't want my insurance company involved. It wasn't my fault. If the boy had watched where he was going, the accident wouldn't have happened."

"Do you have a figure for the costs to settle if a law suit materializes? And there will be a law suit."

"I guess the hospital will have to be paid and the bicycle replaced. Couple thousand for medical and a hundred for the bicycle. Lord knows how much pain, suffering, and 'permanent disability' his folks will claim. You know how these things roll."

"That's not much money. My advice is to go ahead and settle and be done with it."

"The accident was not my fault, and I refuse to pay."

"Suit yourself, but as your attorney I advise you to settle at the first hint of a court action."

Carolyn looked at Matt sharply. "The last time I checked, lawyers served at the pleasure of their clients. My pleasure is to fight this thing as if a million dollars were at stake."

"Then I am officially commissioned to represent you?"

"Of course, you are. I am well aware of how good you are in a courtroom, remember?" Matt did not respond to the question.

"OK. We'll see what happens. Let me know the minute you hear something."

Carolyn called Matt a few times over the next several days. She wanted to see him, but he made excuses to avoid her.

Meanwhile, the philosopher was still in the hospital. Matt and Florence visited him every day, and Hannah went with them on days that she could work around her school schedule. Matt, along with Florence, Hannah, and Melody, returned to the former schedule of church and Sunday afternoons at Florence's house.

"I told you once that I would someday tell you about Brenda Lynne." Florence and the girls had cleared the table and loaded the dishwasher. They joined Matt on the deck, enjoying the April sunshine and soft breezes and waving to tourists walking or driving by. Quiet prevailed for a long time. Finally, Florence broke the silence.

"Brenda Lynne was my daughter."

Matt turned sharply to look at Florence. "I thought you told me once you had never been married. 'Old maid' I believe was the term you used to describe yourself."

"Did I say anything about being married, sonny?" Florence shot back at him. "No, I did not. Now keep quiet if you want to hear the story."

"Yes, ma'am. I do want to know about your daughter, and I will be quiet." Matt pretended repentance; Hannah and Melody concealed smiles at Florence's reprimand of the big, bad New York City attorney.

"She was a beautiful child, Africasian with big, beautiful brown eyes, and skin the color and smoothness of polished brass."

"Africasian?" Matt couldn't resist the impulse to ask.

"That's right, sonny. Do you think I'm going to refer to my daughter as a 'mulatto'? Now hold your peace and let me finish the story."

"Yes, ma'am. Sorry."

"Well, at least you are learning some manners with those 'yes ma'ams.'"

Hannah and Melody covered their mouths to hide stifled laughter. Florence leaned back in her chair and continued her story.

"She was beautiful, smart, and talented. Before she finished high school, she was an accomplished artist. She was anticipating studies at SCAD." Florence paused and looked at Matt. "For you, New York City lawyer, that means Savannah College of Art and Design."

"Yes, ma'am. I'm aware of that." When Florence gave him a stern look, Matt mumbled a sheepish apology for interrupting.

"She looked at other good schools, of course. Ringling in Florida would have been closer to home. But she was fascinated by things she had read about Savannah. She wanted to attend school here. The night after graduation from high school, she was celebrating with three classmates. It wasn't until afternoon of the next day that their bodies were discovered in a thirty-foot canal. Somehow the young lady driving the car—her graduation present—lost control on a winding road. None of them survived." Florence grew silent for a long time as if trying to forget dredged-up pain from a distant time.

"Carl was on a tour of duty in Korea when Brenda Lynne was born. He was a sergeant in the army. We had been together for three years then. We had plans to get married, but who would issue a license to a mixed-race couple in Florida in the early 1950s?" Florence's eyes grew moist and streaked with red. She sat silent for a long time. When she was ready, she cleared her throat and continued her story.

"Carl was leading his platoon on a mission, marching out in front, of course. That was the way he was. The land mine took parts of both legs and his right arm. He lost a lot of blood, but they thought he would survive. They said he could have. But

Carl couldn't face life unable to do all the things he wanted to do with and for his family—especially a new daughter that he had never seen or held in his arms. I guess I should say 'arm.' He gave up after leaving an order that his coffin not be opened.

"Things were hard after Carl's death. The grief was bad enough, but we weren't married, so his benefits were not available to us. Brenda Lynne and I struggled along and did OK, but not great. She was looking forward to finishing her education and making a lot of money to make our lives better. I guess God had a need for a few more angels, so he called her and her friends home to be with him. He didn't realize, I reckon, how hurt those of us left behind would be."

Florence silently stared into the bright afternoon. A minute or two passed, and finally a feeling of well-being settled over her, with the comfort of knowing she was with friends who respected and accepted her without criticism or judgment. They even loved her. She could feel it.

Melody and Hannah sniffed quietly. Robert listened attentively. Matt propped his head in his hands, elbows anchored on his knees, and stared at the floor.

The conversation finally began again and turned to local events. Of particular interest was the Bummers Parade that would occur next month. Matt was not familiar with the event and learned something new about the quirkiness of his new home.

Florence had regained her composure. "It's a parade and a celebration," she explained, "associated with the world's biggest water fight. Everyone on Tybee has a weapon loaded with water, and everyone is a target. If you new comers don't want to get wet, stay indoors during the parade."

In late afternoon the group went their separate ways. Matt walked to the pavilion to listen to the music of local talent. Melody and Hannah donned bikinis and sat on the beach, until the sun began to slide toward the tall pines on Little Tybee. Melody stood and took Hannah's hand and pulled her to her feet.

"Come on. I want to show you something." They walked along the ocean shore to Tybee River and sat on the sea wall built by WPA workers back in the dark days of the 1930's. They lost themselves in girl talk and watched the sun until it dropped out of sight.

"That was a breath-taking sight. Thank you for the show." The afternoon wore on, and Hannah began to see in Melody a kindred spirit, and the two women connected in a way neither expected. Over the next few weeks, they would develop a friendship and bond that would grow, and Hannah would make the decision to enroll in a nursing program when she graduated from high school.

Matt leaned over the rail of the pier watching the two women walking toward him along the beach talking and laughing like old friends. His attention focused on Melody. Watching her in the blue bikini against the white sand of the beach, awareness of a beauty he had previously refused to see awakened in his mind. "What a fool I've been," he murmured aloud.

A tourist nearby overheard and said, "Excuse me?" Matt, embarrassed, looked at the young woman.

"Oh, nothing, nothing. Sorry. I just saw something I've never seen before."

"A sea animal?"

"No. Nothing like that. Just something very special."

"Was it me?' The girl laughed. It was obvious she wanted to keep the conversation going.

Matt returned the laugh. "No, no. Excuse me. Enjoy your visit." He walked away.

He had some thinking to do.

Later that night Florence knelt to say her customary bed-time prayers. In her usual exhortation for forgiveness of sins committed in the day, she realized expletives had not been in her vocabulary all afternoon. She opened her eyes and looked up. "My goodness, that was easy," she said aloud.

From that moment forward, without conscious effort, Florence never again spoke an off-colored word, even at the occasional times she became angry or upset. She finished her prayers and went to bed for a night of sleep more peaceful than any she could remember.

# *Sixteen*

$\mathcal{M}$att was in his office reading the morning paper when the phone rang. He picked it up.

"The doctors have done all they can for John, Matt. They think he will be more comfortable in a homier atmosphere." It was Melody. "They want to dismiss him. Where will he go, Matt? I'm worried."

"I don't know, baby." *Did he call Melody "baby?"* She seemed not to notice.

"We've got to do something, Matt. He can't go back to the bridge."

"Well, what about the mission?"

"Oh, Matt, we can't do that. He needs someone to take care of him."

"Maybe Florence will take him in. Robert, of course, will have to go along to help out. Florence couldn't handle the task alone."

"Can you talk to her? She would probably be more open to the move if you asked."

"I will speak with her about it, but right now I'm going to run up to the hospital to see what John and Robert think about our idea. I'll look you up when I get there. Maybe we should talk to them together. John has fallen in love with you, you know."

"Oh, Matt, nobody loves me."

"Everybody loves you, darling." *Did he call Melody "darling?"* Maybe she won't notice. After all, everyone in Savannah seemed to address everyone else as darlin' or sweetie or some other term of endearment. "Didn't you receive that Daisy Award for outstanding nursing performance?"

"I was lucky. There were others more deserving than me. But if what you say is true, maybe everyone except the one that matters most loves me. What do you think?"

Matt knew well the meaning of Melody's question. He had been aware of her love for a long time. A man knows when he is loved. He can see it and feel it and smell it and taste it with not a word spoken. Women, on the other hand, need the words—often. But Matt would not speak them to Melody, at least not yet—maybe never.

"Maybe you are right. See you in a bit."

The usual greetings and inquiries about health ended, and Matt spoke to the issue at hand.

"John, we've got to get you out of here. Melody and I have a suggestion. You've met our friend, Florence. I'm sure she would be happy to have two strong, handsome, intelligent men move in with her. We haven't spoken to her yet, but we're sure she would be open to the idea."

"Oh, no. No, no. I don't think we could stand that cursing old biddy, and I don't think she could stand us."

Melody could not sit still for that remark. "But she doesn't curse anymore. And, John, you know in your heart that she is a sweet old lady."

"All you women stick together. You think all of y'all are sweet, and even when you don't, you pretend to when men are around."

"Now, John, that's not true and you know it. You're just being crotchety. You need help, and the people that love you are here to offer whatever you need."

"If I were a rude, cursing man, I would say bull shit. But I'm not rude and I don't curse, so I'm just going to say 'baloney.'"

"You're a smart man, John, but you're not smart enough to slip that past us. You are being rude and you cursed." Melody hoped her flippancy would win him over.

"Yes I did, darling, and I'm sorry. But I have a better idea. Why don't we move in with you?"

"John Marion Wayne, you know I couldn't control myself with two handsome men like you and Robert in my little ol' apartment. Besides, I only have one bedroom."

"That sounds good to me. What do you think, Robert, a threesome every night?" Robert offered an uncomfortable laugh and shook his head. He had never heard the philosopher joke like that. His dark face turned darker and everyone knew he was blushing. He looked at Melody and her amused demeanor let him know that everything was cool.

"All right, guys, enough of this foolishness. Matt and I are going to talk to Florence and that's that."

"Now, Melody, you know we can't impose on that old lady," John remarked.

"And I don't know about living in the house with two white women," Robert inserted. "It may be 2012, but this is still the South, you know. What will the neighbors think? Worse still, what will they do? I'm too young and pretty to be strung up on a palm tree. Besides, every time I've visited Tybee I saw hardly any brothers and sisters at all."

"Then you've never been here on Orange Crush Weekend," Melody responded.

"What's an Orange Crush? Sounds like a soda I used to get at the corner store when I was a boy."

"It's a tradition started by Savannah State College students back when it was an all-black school. A lot of the kids couldn't afford to go to the Bahamas or Aruba of even Florida on spring break. So, a group of them got together and spent the weekend on Tybee. As time went by, the numbers grew.

"Their school colors are reflex blue and burnt orange. So there you have it: Orange Crush Weekend. In recent years—usually in May—not only the regional, but black students from all around the country choose the island for spring break. Unfortunately, some visitors who are not students come hoping to make time with the young co-eds and maybe peddle drugs. That sometimes creates disturbances, but you won't have any problems. Most of the conflicts are among themselves," Melody explained.

John broke in. "You don't need to worry, son, about living with those beautiful white women. There's not a palm tree in Chatham County strong enough to break that neck of yours. And, yes, you are relatively young, but 'pretty' is too big of a stretch for a normal imagination." Everyone laughed. It appeared to Matt that John was working hard to lighten a heavy situation.

"And listen, boy—and I'll call you 'boy' if I want to. I'm a dying man. And in case you've forgotten, you're my best friend. And I and my best friend are moving in with a beautiful white woman and a crotchety old cursing something-or-other—if they will have us."

"Let me go then, guys," Matt said, relieved that the issue was settled. "I'll get with Florence and let you know what she says."

"Of course they can come here with me and Hannah. We'd love to have a couple of men in the house. And Robert can help out with the things that have long needed fixing around here."

"Your expenses will increase some, Florence: food, water, and electricity, and such. But John has money. He'll be happy to help out," Matt said.

"That won't be a big problem. Hannah is already helping a little with some of the allowance she gets from her conservator every month."

"Thanks, Florence. Melody and I really appreciate your gracious attitude. By the way, how is Hannah doing?"

"She's doing great. She goes to school and comes home. That's her daily routine. She's stopped talking to all those boys that call her, and she has made application to the nursing program."

"That's wonderful. Has she said anything about moving out?"

"Not a word. I don't think that's going to happen. She and Melody are such great pals now. And she loves the island. She's found a home, Matt."

"You called me by my name. What happened to 'sonny'?"

"I'm beginning to like you—sonny.

"Thanks, Florence. I love you, too."

"Get out of here—sonny. I've got to make preparations for two guests. Pick Melody up, and y'all come to supper. Hannah may be home by then, too."

Matt walked away.

"Melody loves you, you know," Florence called after him.

Matt kept walking and did not look back.

# Seventeen

*T*he next morning Matt went to his office and checked the day's newspapers. He was enjoying himself and had little ambition to be interrupted, not even by a paying client. The phone rang and he ignored it. When he finished with the news, he punched the "play" button on the answering machine. He had two calls. He listened to the first one. The caller had been cited for walking his dog on the beach and was threatened by a fine of five hundred dollars. He protested that he was exercising his dog after dark at low tide. Only a handful of beach-goers were out to be bothered by his dog; and even if the animal pooped on the beach, which the caller said he would not allow, come high tide it would disappear.

"Can you help me, Mr. Ryan?" the caller pleaded.

Matt called the man back immediately. "Sorry, dude, can't help you with this one. Rules are rules. Are you familiar with the dog park up at the north end?"

The man answered in the affirmative. "But I didn't want to drive my car. You know how expensive gas is."

"Indeed I do, but it's cheaper than a fine for breaking the rules. Sorry, pal. Can't help you. Good luck. Plead your case. Maybe you can catch a break."

"Go to hell, man. You probably helped them make the rule." The caller hung up before he could hear Matt chuckle.

He punched in the other message and immediately recognized Carolyn's voice. He could tell she was upset. He wondered if he was the object of her discomfort. He had not seen or called her in a while. He had to return her call, but he hesitated, dreading what or who her problem could be. He stared at the phone. What was he going to tell her? He had been busy? She knew better. He had been sitting with a dying friend? He couldn't tell her that. A lecture about wasting time with riff-raff would surely follow. She couldn't understand his relationship with those homeless people anyway.

He continued staring at the phone for several minutes. He covered his face with both hands. A feeling of unrest and uneasiness descended heavily upon him. Conflicting thoughts darted painfully through his heart and mind, and he did not want them there. He wanted to be comfortable with loving Carolyn, and he wanted with all his heart for her to love him.

His first love, like all first loves, was hard to forget. The thought of what if remains in the deep recesses of the heart forever. And once a love becomes comfortable, it is hard to give it up. Other what ifs may come along: the long eye contact from the girl at the end of the bar, the waitress's phone number on the credit card receipt, the smile from the car in the next lane of stalled traffic. But through it all, a first love remains tightly woven in the fabric of the lover's being.

After a long while, he gave in and dialed Carolyn's number.

"The little twerp and his family have done it, Matt. They've filed a lawsuit." Carolyn was more upset than he thought she should be. The minor nature of the accident and the financial settlement could not be as bad as she seemed to think.

"Their lawyer called me this morning. And of all the lawyers in Chatham County, Bruce Bradley is handling the case for them. They wanted to file a suit in Superior Court, but after Bruce told them the case would not be heard for possibly a year or longer, and after that even more time to be settled, they opted to go with a small claim in magistrate court. The hospital is pushing them for payment and they want to get the case settled and over with."

Matt interrupted her. "A small claim can't possibly be that bad. What is the limit in Georgia?"

"They haven't talked about an amount yet, but it could be as much as fifteen thousand. Bruce is a friend. I play tennis with him and his wife, Corinne, so that's a good thing."

*That poor kid doesn't stand a chance,* Matt thought. "I'll contact Bruce and see what I can do."

"Why don't you come by the house tonight and let me know what you found out."

"I wish I could, but I've got an urgent issue that needs all the attention I can give it," Matt lied. "I'll see if I can connect with the kid's lawyer and call you later."

"I haven't seen much of you lately, Matt. I miss you." The sweetness in Carolyn's voice inched its way into the confused and tender edges of his emotions. Memories began to evolve in his heart and mind. How could he not love her for all the good times of their youth?

"I miss you, too. Maybe I can shift some priorities around and come by later."

"That'll be great. I can't wait to see you again. I have really missed you, Matt."

"About eight?"

"Eight sounds great." Carolyn laughed. "I'm a poet."

"That you are. A rhyming poet even."

" By the way, how is Hannah doing?"

"She's doing well. She graduates next month, and she has applied to nursing school."

"Well, I'll be damned. Who would have thought it?"

Carolyn was beginning to sound like herself. Matt did not want to hear her go there. He needed to hold on to the memory in his mind, and he had become fond of the young woman Hannah was becoming. "She's making a lot of progress in her life. She's even given up all her boyfriends. You will be proud of her."

"I doubt that."

Matt would not listen to any more of Carolyn's criticism. "See you at eight." He hung up the phone without waiting for a response. "Why in hell did I agree to go over there tonight?" Matt said aloud. "Damn!"

He picked up the phone and dialed Bruce Bradley.

"I'm going for the max, Matthew. I don't know what the judge will do, probably nothing near the fifteen grand. But spectators will be in the courtroom and I've got to make a showing. I have to make a living, you know. And I have a reputation to protect."

"You don't have much of a case, Bruce. Carolyn says the boy actually ran into her."

"That's not what the boy says. He is going to testify that she veered off the traffic lane and struck him. He may even insinuate that she did it deliberately. You and I know, of course, that didn't happen, but once the thought is out there, the judge will have to consider the possibility. I'm going to push hard, Matthew. You've got to be on your game. I don't think I have anything to worry about at all. I see it as a slam-dunk."

"I think you are wrong, and my game will be ready, Mr. Bradley. You just make sure you get a good night's sleep before the trial."

"See you then, sport."

"Yeah." The last thing Matt heard before he hung up the phone was Bruce's laughter. *I'm going to whitewash that bastard's ass just for the hell of it.*

Carolyn was waiting for Matt when he arrived. She met him at the door and threw her arms around him and embraced him tightly for a long time. It appeared that some of the old Carolyn was back. Her welcome left him feeling light headed and weightless on his feet. If one of the infamous Savannah thunderstorms with their strong winds blew up at that moment, he knew for sure he would be swept away.

Carolyn finally slid her arms from around his neck. She took him by the hand and led him toward the bedroom. Matt followed without comment or question, except in his own mind.

*What is she up to? Is she playing a game, or is her need great and I am conveniently at hand?*

In the bedroom she sat him on the bed and began taking off his shoes. When that was done, she pushed him back on the bed and loosened his belt. She grasped the waist of his pants and began working them off his body, all the while maintaining eye contact with him as he lay silently watching, wondering what next. With her eyes still focused on his, she pulled him upright and removed his shirt. When he was almost nude, she backed away and began a slow suggestive dance, movements Cleopatra would envy.

"I'm going to get undressed while you tell me what you found out." Staring into Matt's eyes, she began removing her clothing one garment at a time.

"Your friend may not be the pal you think he is," Matt began. "He said he's going for blood."

Carolyn stopped her striptease abruptly. "That perverted leech!" Her eyes narrowed and her face tightened and turned dark. "I should have known he couldn't be trusted. I'll bet he has told everybody about that little roll in the St. Augustine we had a couple of years ago. He wants more, but I keep turning him down. Now he's going to get back at me, and there's nothing I can do about it."

Matt listened to that revelation and the swelling inside his white Munsingwear briefs began to deflate. *Why in hell did she have to tell me that?* It seemed to him a strange mix of justice was unfolding here. But stranger things had transpired here in the city, like the case where a grand juror sat on a panel considering a murder indictment against himself.

"You've been with Bradley?"

"Oh, Matt, it was nothing. One time, a long time ago. And I assure you, it was nothing. The arrogant pervert was over and done before I knew he had started."

"Was that before the tennis match with his wife or after?"

Carolyn recognized the anger in Matt's voice. "Are we going to fight over something that happened before you came to Savannah? I told you it was nothing."

"I doubt that Corinne would see it as nothing."

"What she doesn't know won't hurt her. Besides, I'm not the only one."

"And that excuses banging your friend's husband?"

"Look, I'm not going to waste a whole evening worrying about a friend's domestic problems." Carolyn returned to the attraction at hand while Matt stared unbelieving into her face showing neither shame nor remorse nor regret. He lay undressed except for his underwear.

Maintaining eye contact with Matt, she removed her shoes one at a time while still standing. She threw herself onto his chest, forcing him back in a supine position on the bed. She pushed his briefs down and found him unresponsive.

"What's wrong?"

Matt answered her question in the manner that all men answer, no matter how many times it has happened.

"I don't know." The second part of the response must follow, but he took a moment to think on their days at Harvard. "This has never happened to me before." Indeed, it had never happened previously. But he was younger then, desperately in love with Carolyn, and his testosterone gauge was registering O for "Overflowing." A railroad spike driven through his business equipment would not have fazed it back then.

Several minutes passed with Carolyn trying to resurrect the lifeless instrument of tonight's entertainment. She tried everything she knew to awaken a response in Matt. She eagerly pursued her mission, and he did not care. It was clear that she needed this thing to happen. When nothing she knew worked, she lay on her back staring at the ceiling. They lay quiet under a blanket of crushing tension for a long time. Matt regretted letting her talk him into tonight's visit. His feelings for her must be inside him somewhere, but at that instance he could not find them no matter how hard he searched. Confused questions swept through his mind like a Tybee Island wind storm, and he could not stop them. On and on they whirled uncontrolled. He was relieved when Carolyn spoke.

"I think you had better go."

"Yeah, sure. I guess I should." He stood up and began to throw on his clothes. The sooner he extricated himself from the situation, the better for him and for her.

"See yourself out. Pull that door there closed, but don't lock the outside door."

"Sure. See you later." He closed the bedroom door behind him, and through the tiny crack before the door closed completely, he paused for a brief moment to see Carolyn reaching for the phone on the table beside the bed.

*The girl has a need, and she won't be denied on this night. I wonder who the poor fool will be.*

He hurried through the house and out the front door. Pulling it shut behind him, he muttered, "Why the hell should I care? I don't give a mariner's damn." He threw himself into the driver's seat of the car. He inserted the key and started the engine. He stopped when he heard the radio playing Lady Antebellum's *Need You Now*. The current time was getting on toward 1a.m., and he knew Carolyn was calling someone to fill the need that he had created in her. He laughed and declared loudly, "Now how ironic is that? Mocked by my own damn radio."

Matt did not see or communicate with Carolyn until the day before the hearing in magistrate court. He dialed her number at the bank. "Don't you think we ought to give the kid a couple thousand and forget this whole matter?"

"Hell no. You are my attorney and you work for me. I'm not giving away a cent that I don't have to. Besides that, we can't lose. An eye witness to the accident came forward today. She is a bank customer. She's ready to testify that the boy ran into me."

"That's great. You won't need me then. It looks like a winner for your side. And let me remind you that I haven't asked you for the first cent. For that price or any price, I advise you to pay the kid a few dollars and forget the hearing."

"Matt, I will be in court in the morning, and I expect you to be there. Don't you even think about abandoning me. If you do, you can bet you will pay dearly. I have influential friends in this town that you've never even heard of."

Matt felt like saying screw you and your influential friends and the royal stallions they rode in on, except that he would prefer to use the word and not the euphemism. That would really get to her. But he was a professional lawyer, and he would maintain professionalism and a rational mind.

After a brief moment to consider a response, he calmly and sternly said, "I have no intentions of letting you go into that courtroom alone, but don't threaten me. I'm not afraid of you or your influential friends."

"You be there ready to argue this case."

The abrupt sound of the phone's receiver slammed onto its cradle rattled in Matt's ear. He could only imagine the rage she was feeling. He almost wished he could be with her now to see it.

# Eighteen

The next morning Matt arrived at the courthouse early with ambivalent feelings about the task before him. He knew the plaintiff would require an award in some amount. He had little enthusiasm for seeing Carolyn win, and he wanted to slam that smart-assed Bruce Bradley, but ethics demanded that he present the best defense possible. Every time he saw Bruce or heard him or thought of him, Matt's mind pictured him and Carolyn in a game more intimate than a tennis match. He hated Bruce for that. And even worse, now the jerk was trying to get a rematch.

The lawyers entered the courtroom and took their respective places. Waiting for the judge, a bailiff and the court reporter exchanged idle banter. A few minutes later, the plaintiff arrived. The kid and his grandmother walked sheepishly to the table where Bruce sat with a smug look on his face. The litigants looked around the room. Fear filled their eyes and masked their faces. They were in a place that held no familiarity to them. They glanced quickly in Matt's direction, but did not make eye contact.

Matt inconspicuously studied their presence and demeanor. The woman wore a one-piece cotton dress showing obvious signs of age and use. The young man wore off-brand jeans and a short-sleeved shirt. Matt guessed they lived in the government projects.

At exactly 10 a.m. the judge entered the courtroom and began the usual procedures. When he had all his notes and documents in place, the judge asked Bruce if he was ready to begin. He turned to Matt and framed the same question. Anxiety rose in his chest. Carolyn was not present, nor had he heard from her. The judge shuffled papers before him, preparing to make a default judgment. Carolyn walked in looking as if it were she who was directing the process. Matt, relieved, rose and replied, "We're ready, Your Honor."

"Thank you, Mr. Ryan. Please advise your client that this is not the only case to be heard today and punctuality is of the essence. Mr. Bradley, present your case."

"Your Honor, we are here to present a clear case of liability. My client, Mr. Charles Jones, was innocently on his way to school, when the defendant drove her car into him while he was riding his bicycle well onto the shoulder of the road. The defendant was engaged in an activity we all have been guilty of from time to time, but with less tragic results. My client could have been seriously injured by the defendant's irresponsibility or even killed. Mrs. Winston was distracted from her driving by something she was reaching for on the floor of her vehicle." Bruce paused to allow that image to permeate the judge's thoughts. Carolyn glared at the attorney with rage flashing from her eyes. Matt touched her arm to calm and constrain her.

"Unfortunately, my client is a penniless schoolboy, Your Honor, and he has hospital expenses he can't pay, and his bicycle was destroyed in the accident. Mrs. Winston was clearly negligent, Your Honor, and for that lapse of judgment, we're praying upon the Court for the maximum award of fifteen thousand dollars." Looking across the room at Carolyn and Matt, the smug expression on Bruce's face intensified with a malicious glow.

"No need for prayer this morning, Mr. Bradley. Save that for your morning devotionals. Pass your client's bills up and let me take a look at them." The judge turned to Matt. "Let's hear from the defendant, Mr. Ryan."

"With the Court's permission, Your Honor, we will present a three-part defense. Defense 1: Plaintiff's Complaint failed to state a specific claim against my client upon which relief may be granted. Defense 2: Plaintiff has failed to present an affidavit of an expert as to damages in this case as required by O.C.GA. S 9-11-9. Defense 3: Plaintiff did, in fact, cause the accident for which Plaintiff seeks relief; therefore, Plaintiff's Complaint must be dismissed."

"Thank you for your eloquent cry, Mr. Ryan, but the Court will determine appropriate action in the plaintiff's complaint." The judge seemed irritated at Matt's use of the word 'must' in his presentation. "I will hear the case, Mr. Ryan. Is there anything else?"

"May I examine the plaintiff, Your Honor?"

"Go ahead, Mr. Ryan." The judge called the boy to the lectern. The young man stood on shaky legs and testified in an unsteady voice that he saw the driver of the car reach for something on the passenger-side floor, and her car darted into his path causing him to strike her vehicle near the rear wheel. He explained further, in a voice becoming more unsteady, that the impact knocked him off his bicycle and the car's rear wheel ran over it, causing damage beyond repair. Matt challenged each of the boy's statements. By the time the interrogation was finished, the boy's voice had become barely audible, but his testimony remained unchanged. The case was not looking good for Carolyn.

"Do you have anything further, Mr. Ryan?"

"Yes, I do, Your Honor. I would like to call the defendant who will testify on her own behalf."

Matt called Carolyn to the stand, and she repeated the story previously presented by her attorney. She apologized to the Court and to the plaintiff, even though the boy himself caused the accident that she in no way could have prevented. She spoke with the most humility and sorrow she could muster. "I've tried to be fair in every way, Your Honor. I have not even asked the Court or the defendant for repairs to the damage done to my car when the young man ran into me."

Following Carolyn's testimony the judge said, "Let's keep the procedure moving. We have several other cases to hear today." He shuffled papers in front of him and looked about the room.

"Anything else, Mr. Ryan?

"With your permission, Your Honor, I do have additional testimony in this case. "I have one more witness."

"Get on with it, Mr. Ryan."

"Judge, this is an unfortunate case where a young man riding his bicycle struck a small stone, or in some other way was thrown off his usual course and happened to veer into Mrs. Winston's car, as she drove to her job as the president of Winston State Bank. We will concede that the young man did receive some minor injuries and damage to his bike, but it was he who caused the accident. We will present an eye witness to testify to these facts. We submit, therefore, that Mrs. Winston should be held harmless in this case, and on Mrs. Winston's behalf ask that the charges be dismissed with prejudice." Matt had given this information to the plaintiff's attorney, but Bruce had shown little interest, so Matt did not reveal what the witness would testify to.

The eye witness, a Mrs. Barlow, looking more nervous than the plaintiffs, testified that she witnessed the bicycle striking the car. Reading from notes on a pad lying on the lectern, she avoided making eye contact with anyone in the courtroom. Matt noted her behavior.

The hearing ended and the judge began deliberating, verbalizing each step as he proceeded.

"It seems to me at first blush that the plaintiff has carried the argument in this case. It seems more reasonable that the defendant's vehicle would more likely veer off the roadway than would the plaintiff's bicycle veer into her. And I noted the plaintiff's demeanor at the lectern. It seems to me he was extremely stressed by appearing here. I'm inclined to believe he would not have made this appearance had he not been convinced of his justification in this matter." The judge paused and opened a folder in front of him. Carolyn looked at Matt with rage building in her eyes. This thing was not looking too good. Matt focused on the judge and paid her no attention.

"On the other hand, however," the judge continued, "comes now an eye witness who also appears to be credible. It seems to the Court then, that liability is shared in this instance. I am going to rule a Vicarious Liability in the case and award the plaintiff two thousand, one hundred forty-seven dollars and sixty-three cents for medical expenses and order that payment be made directly to the hospital. I will also direct a payment of five hundred dollars be paid to Mr. Bradley. No additional damages are awarded. That is my verdict. Have a good day, ladies and gentlemen."

Carolyn took a deep breath and smiled and walked with Matt from the courtroom. "We did it Matt." Carolyn's sense of victory shone in her eyes and glowed on her face. "I've got to get over to the bank now, but let's get together this evening and celebrate. Can we do that?" Without waiting for an answer, she rose on her toes and kissed Matt's cheek. She then quickly disappeared down the hallway.

The afternoon passed quickly and Matt picked Carolyn up at her home. At her direction, they frequented most of the hot spots in Savannah. By 10 p.m. the jubilant Carolyn was finding it difficult to maintain balance and stand upright. Against her protests Matt took her home. He intended to put her to bed and head out to the island. Maybe Melody would still be up and about, and he would hang out with her a while.

But Carolyn changed his plans. After he had undressed her and put her to bed, she pulled him down beside her and began clumsily removing his clothing. He did not help, neither did he resist. When they were both undressed, he enjoyed Carolyn more than any time since their reconciliation. She made love to him in every way a woman could love a man. When they both were exhausted, they fell asleep in Carolyn's bed with no protest at all that he go home.

The next morning they awoke around noon. Carolyn complained of a headache and called the bank to report that she was ill, a touch of flu maybe, and would not be in today. She would not need to call Mona, her maid/assistant. Today was her usual day off.

The couple made love through the afternoon, and when the shadows crawled from under the trees and shrubbery into open spaces on the east side of the house, Carolyn eased out of bed and wrapped herself in a robe. "Call me tomorrow," she said over her shoulder and disappeared into the bathroom.

Matt got out of bed and quickly threw on enough clothes to get him home and into his own shower. He would have been happy to share Carolyn's, but she had dismissed him, and protest would be useless.

Nevertheless, he went away with a smile on his face, thinking that he had enjoyed just compensation for all the misery and indignities she had put him through in past months. But tomorrow she would be sober and the Carolyn he was struggling to love. He had tried to love her, tried hard. He had gambled that he could love her into the Carolyn of an earlier day. But every gambler knows when to fold and leave the table. Maybe the time had come for him to store the memories of his last hours with Carolyn in a comfortable and cozy pocket of his heart and take a long walk.

# Nineteen

$\mathcal{M}$att hung out on the island for the next several days. Evenings were spent walking on the beach and Back River with Melody. On Sunday he went to church with her, Florence, and her house guests. A hardy lunch, as always, followed church. After the kitchen clean-up, they congregated for several hours of lounging on Florence's front deck. Matt settled into a chair, thinking about the number of times Carolyn had called him and the excuses he had made to avoid her. The last time he had been with her was fantastic, but past experience had taught him that her moods could quickly change, and she would eventually dump him, and she would have her ultimate revenge. If he could stick to a decision to never see her again, their last night together would be a memory to treasure, a memory that may erase all the pain she had piled on him since they reconnected.

John was still strong enough to attend church with the group by using Florence's wheelchair. The filling of her home with activity, excitement, and love had her feeling much better and her arthritis less worrisome.

Eating caused pain in John's stomach. He subsisted on nutrition drinks and sweet iced tea, and kept the conversation going with his philosophies of life in general. Most of his observations were accepted, some tolerated, and some downright explosive, attracting serious debate from one or all of the rest of the group. One of the most virulent debates followed his contention that terminally ill patients should have the right to end their life in the way they choose. He argued that it makes no sense for loved ones to be obligated to endure the pain of watching a slow death, while the patient suffers the indignity of being the focus of the death watch. "If I can manage to hang on to my dignity while living under a bridge, surely I deserve the right to die with dignity on this island in this beautiful house, and y'all certainly deserve to be relieved of suffering through my drawn-out passing."

The fiercest uproar ever followed that treatise until Florence finally demanded, "Hush it up. Stop it. There will be no more talk of dying."

"But I am going to die, you know."

Florence gave John a stern look. "I said stop it. There will be no more talk of dying."

And there wasn't. At least, not for a while.

On Monday morning Matt sat in his office pondering strategy in the DUI case the client insisted he and he alone take. He assumed it was a dilemma most criminal defense lawyers face from time to time. Evidence often indicates the defendant's guilt, but it's the attorney's duty to vindicate the client, or get the best deal possible. In his practice of corporate law, usually it was only money at stake, and his clients had plenty to work with. He never felt bad about taking it from one or giving it to another. But in defending crime—no matter how large or small—the defendants' lives in some measure are at stake.

His current client, a local college student, had no previous DUI arrests. He had visited the island on the weekend of spring break and let the revelry get out of hand. Matt would give him a stern lecture—sure to be followed by the judge's reprimand—and attempt to get him off with a stiff fine and community service. His parents were not wealthy, so the young man would have to come up with the money on his own. He had a job waiting tables at a restaurant in the city, and all his earnings would go to the Tybee court for some time. He would also have to pay Matt's fee, which was set at the usual rate, with no mercy shown the young man. That should teach him a strong lesson to leave the driving to others the next time he decided to overdose on the vine.

His strategy deliberations were interrupted by the ringing telephone. He lifted the receiver.

"Mr. Ryan?"

"Yes, ma'am." Matt had quickly gotten comfortable with the southern mannerisms that seemed to come natural to him now.

"Mr. Ryan, I don't have money to pay you, but I need your help."

"I'll do whatever I can." The voice sounded familiar.

"What's the problem, ma'am?"

"This is Peggy Barlow, Mr. Ryan, and when I tell you the purpose of this phone call, you may want to call me Lying Peggy Barlow."

"I'm sure I wouldn't do that, Mrs. Barlow."

"Well, thank you for that sir. I'm a liar, Mr. Ryan, and I can't live with that."

"I can't help you with bad habits, ma'am. Maybe you ought to see your pastor."

"It's your help I need. You see, I was in court the day you defended Mrs. Winston in the accident with that child on the bicycle. I lied, Mr. Ryan. I saw the accident, but that's not the way it happened."

"Oh? Can you tell me about it? Tell me why you lied?"

"Yes, sir, I intend to do just that. My son came back from Afghanistan recently. He's stationed with the Third ID over at Fort Benning in Columbus, Georgia. That's what they call it, the Third ID, but it means Third Infantry Division—"

"Yes, ma'am. I'm aware of that," Matt interrupted. He needed to get back to the DUI case.

"Well anyway, he came to see me when he came back, but his leave time is limited, you know."

"Yes ma'am. I'm aware of that."

"He's the only kin I have left, Mr. Ryan, and I get terrible lonesome to see him sometimes. I went to see Mrs. Winston to borrow five thousand dollars to buy a used car. My neighbor said he was buying one of those zippy little cars that run on electricity. By the way, Mr. Ryan, I've never seen one of those things in motion. Do you know how they keep the power cords plugged in while they are zipping around in those little electric cars?"

"Well, ma'am, I don't think they do it that way. I believe most of them use a combination of batteries and the usual gasoline engines."

"Oh, well now. That makes perfect sense when you think about it. Anyway, my neighbor had a car he wanted to sell. It looked good and he says he hasn't driven it much. I never can remember the name of it. I know it's a Ford—a princess or queen or something."

Matt interrupted her. "Is it a Ford Crown Victoria?"

"Yes, sir. I believe that's it. A Crown Victoria."

"That's a reliable car." Matt wanted to hurry her along. "Did you get the money to buy the car, Mrs. Barlow?"

"Yes, I did. Runs like a top. I used to hear my Fred say that about his Chevy before he wrecked it. Died in the crash. It was so sad. My boy had just turned twelve then."

"I'm sorry."

"Thank you Mr. Ryan. I can tell you have a kind heart. Anyway, Mrs. Winston didn't want to give me the money because I live on Social Security and all. She told me she couldn't sue if I didn't pay. I told her my son would help with the payments, but that still didn't matter she said. I started to leave, and I happened to mention I saw the accident and hoped everyone came out OK. Just like that, Mr. Ryan, her whole attitude changed. She acted so nice. She asked me to sit down, and she had this pretty young thing bring me a cup of coffee with cream and sugar and everything just the way I make it on my Mister Coffee at home. My coffee is one thing I really enjoy, Mr. Ryan, especially on cool mornings. Sometimes when I get my housework done and all, I have a cup of coffee with cream and sugar and watch local

TV. You know something, Mr. Ryan? I tried a little box of that Splenda one time—I'm a little stout, you know—and the price of that stuff is so high. It's good, but I can't afford to buy that again—."

By now Matt's lawyer instinct was pounding in his brain like up close at a Fourth of July fireworks show. He knew where Mrs. Barlow was headed. He didn't want to be rude, but he couldn't wait for her to get to the heart of her story. "The change in Mrs. Winston's attitude, tell me about that, Mrs. Barlow"

"Yes, sir, let me tell you about that."

"Please do."

"Well, sir, Mrs. Winston had a coffee, too. She just sat there for a long time rocking real slow in that big chair with this funny expression on her face, peering over the top of that nice cup she was sipping from. I didn't know what else to do, so I sat there drinking my coffee while Mrs. Winston sipped hers with that funny look on her face. I kind of wanted her to hurry up so I could get back home to watch my program. That program 'The Price is Right.' Do you ever watch that show, Mr. Ryan? These contestants win stuff and all and they get so excited..."

"I've seen that program, Mrs. Barlow, but tell me about your meeting with Mrs. Winston."

"Yes, sir. I need to do that. Well, half way through my coffee, she finally said something. She said she might be able to make the loan after all, if I was sure I could make the payments and help her out a little."

"Oh, my God, Mrs. Barlow. She didn't, and you didn't?"

"Yes, sir. I'm sorry to say I did. She told me what to say, and you heard me say it. Just as plain as you please, I lied right there in front of that poor child and you and the judge. And I'm sure God heard me and was not at all pleased with what Lying Peggy Barlow did."

"Oh, my God," Matt repeated.

"What I did was pretty bad wasn't it, Mr. Ryan? Now I've got to figure out a way to get my neighbor's car back to him and get the money to take back to Mrs. Winston. Can you help me with that, Mr. Ryan?"

Matt didn't speak for a long moment. He couldn't believe Carolyn would stoop that low.

"Mr. Ryan?"

"Yes, ma'am, I'm here. I think I can help you, Mrs. Barlow. I think we can work this out without your having to return the car."

"You lawyers are always so smart, Mr. Ryan. But will it be right for me to keep the car and Mrs. Winston's money? And what about that poor child's bicycle?

"I can fix this, Mrs. Barlow. Don't you worry about it. I want you to keep making your payments to the bank, and I'll take care of the rest."

"Thank you Mr. Ryan. You lawyers are always so smart. I'm sorry I don't have money to pay you."

"That's all right, Mrs. Barlow. Go see your son every chance you get, and tell him I said thanks for his service."

"I will tell him, Mr. Ryan, and thank you for your service. You lawyers are always so smart."

"Good bye, Mrs. Barlow."

Matt locked his office and drove immediately to the courthouse. He went to the Magistrate's office and found the address of Charles Jones, the victim in the accident. He drove to a bicycle shop and selected a red Schwinn Cruiser complete with a light for seeing on the front and a red light for being seen on the back. He paid the merchant and rolled the bike to his car and lifted it into the trunk. He made a quick stop at the ATM then drove to Charles Jones' home and knocked on the door. Matt was pleased to find the boy's home a small, neat single-family residence, not a project house at all. The grandmother answered the knock and informed Matt that Charles was in his room working on school assignments. She was suspicious of the lawyer, but finally agreed to call her grandson out. Charles walked cautiously to the front door.

"Come out to the yard, son. I have something for you." The boy looked at Matt without moving. He gave his grandmother a questioning look. Only when she smiled and motioned him onward did he follow Matt.

When Charles saw the new bicycle, a smile lit his face like a sudden burst of sunshine on an overcast day. Without disclosing details that would fall negatively on others involved in the case, Matt explained that mistakes had been made and apologized for his role in the outcome of the trial. The boy mounted the bicycle and made a few doughnuts on the Saint Augustine grass carpeting the yard. Satisfied that the bike was quality, he braked in front of Matt and thanked him again. Matt slipped a one hundred dollar bill into the pocket of the boy's jeans. "Take this to help you with school expenses," Matt told him. After several more "thank you's" from Charles, Matt drove back to the island.

Instead of going directly to his office, he drove to Florence's house and found Robert and John sitting on the front deck. The philosopher listened intently as Matt told the entire story. When he had finished, the three men sat silent for several minutes. Without looking at Matt, the philosopher broke the silence. "You know, barrister, I might live long enough to learn to like you."

Matt fumbled deliberately in his shirt pocket and finally took out a pen and a small notepad. Robert looked on with a quizzical expression covering his face. Matt began to write. John's curiosity could wait no longer. "What the hell are you writing?"

"I want to make sure I don't forget to include that in your eulogy. 'John Wayne almost liked me.' When the time comes, I want to recall those words pretty much verbatim. They may be enough to get you past St. Peter."

John leaned his head against the back of the chair and closed his eyes. "Go to hell, barrister."

Matt and Robert laughed.

## Twenty

*T*he slow and easy days of spring edged forward basking each day with more warmth and comfort than the day before. Spring breakers first came in March and were coming still in May, noted most obviously by the Orange Crush Weekend students, and the drug dealers and stalkers following them hoping to take their money or their bodies or both, leaving behind litter—and embarrassment—for Savannah State University and her decent students conforming to the rules of civility. African-Americans ordinarily do not visit the island in large numbers. They have little need for tanning, so their visits are for pier or surf fishing, for enjoying special events, or for splashing in the ocean, usually when late afternoon has cooled a bit.

Sunscreen-lathered, bikinied bodies now carpeted the beach leaving barely walking room on the sand.

At about the same time, around Memorial Day, the Beach Bum Parade—also known as the world's biggest water fight—is staged. Water guns large and small come out on the day of the parade. Everyone except, of course, police officers and other emergency officials—is a likely target for a drenching. Obvious tourists in full dress are most often given a free pass. One unfortunate visitor—as luck would have it, a college coed unfamiliar with the rules—made the mistake of dowsing a police officer. Matt pleaded her case and got her off with a fine and an apology.

Matt had not seen Carolyn since the day her court case was settled. She called from time to time, but he ignored the calls. The messages she always left grew more vitriolic with the passing days. After a while he decided he could do without that kind of abuse and erased them without listening. With the disintegration of his relationship with Carolyn, he now had more time to spend with Melody and Florence's household, and he took advantage of it.

John's condition continued to deteriorate. His weight plummeted to ninety-seven pounds. It became obvious to everyone that he would soon be leaving them. He exerted all the energy he could muster into his passing with dignity. He made it a point to do as much for himself as he could. To his dismay—and despite his protests—Florence, Melody, Hannah, and Robert fussed over him. "Dammit, can't y'all see I can do this on my own?" was the only complaint heard from him—and that often. Robert dragged himself through the days in a stupor of fear and grieving. He would miss his first real friend since his mother passed, and he worried about his fate without John. He suddenly realized how much he had come to depend on the philosopher.

John worried about how his final arrangements would be paid for. He didn't want charity, but he didn't want to be buried in an undignified pauper's grave. "As a matter of fact," he said to the group on a Sunday afternoon, "I don't want to be buried at all. I don't like the idea of my body lying in a cold, damp tomb deteriorating slowly. I would much rather get it over with quickly. If I had my wishes, I would be cremated and my ashes spread in the Atlantic, preferably in the gulfstream. The urn I would like placed with this lady right here." He weakly patted Florence's knee.

"She, I would hope, would keep it right here in this house for as long as she is alive." John grew silent for a couple of minutes. In deep thought he massaged the arms of his chair with the palms of his hands. "Sort of like my friend, Robert, it's been a long time since I've felt a belonging. This lady here, and this family gathered here, welcomed me into this house and changed that. Until now I have always felt suspended alone in space like Plato's images on the cave wall. The only realities I recall since Anna is this family here, and also like my friend Robert, recognition of the creator of the universe." He pulled his body up as straight as he could in his chair, and winced. When the pain subsided, he continued.

"Unfortunately, we are not born into reality. We have not a clue what we're doing here. We trust that question will be answered in the hereafter. But reality here must be created. I've learned we do that through culture, love of family, love of our fellow man, and humility before our creator. That's what we do. We take breath, motility, heart, and intellect and mold them into what we recognize as reality." John again paused as another wave of pain wrenched his body. When the pain subsided, thoughtful silence took him again. The others quietly waited, instinctively aware that he was not through speaking. The long silence ended, and he began in a soft voice that seemed to be verbalized thinking. Everyone strained to hear.

"It has been written that 'young men shall see visions, old men shall dream dreams.' I don't know which I'm supposed to be, but this morning while y'all were at church, I dozed off sitting here in this chair. I had a dream or a vision or a hallucination, and a spirit came to me and got right in my face and said, 'Do you want me to pray for you?' and I said 'yes.' It asked me again twice more and my answers were 'yes.' And I asked, 'What are you going to pray for? I don't particularly want to live. What is your prayer?' He didn't answer. And I looked beyond the spirit and on the right was my father dressed in fine clothes stitched with gold thread. He wore dress shoes, beautiful shoes trimmed in gold, and he was smiling and beckoning to me and nodding his head and he looked rested and happy.

"On the left my mother's usually bound hair fell around her shoulders, and it was streaked with gold. She wore a white robe trimmed in crimson lace and was smiling and dancing about. I have never seen her dance before. She never believed in dancing. She called my name, and I followed them, and a feeling of euphoria came upon me, and I was free and I was happy.

"We danced down a long, dim tunnel, and at the end, a light shone brighter than the clearest summer solstice ever seen on the island here or anywhere. And my parents gathered me in their arms and they had tears in their eyes and they were saying, 'Son, we're sorry. Maybe there was something better we could have done, but we didn't know. We just didn't know.'"

Tears welled in all the eyes of the people gathered around John. A few sniffles were heard, but no one looked at the other for fear of outright weeping. John would not like that.

"I looked beyond my mother and father and I saw a man in a white robe. He had long auburn hair and a beard, and a porcelain-clear face glowing as if lit by a powerful light from within. He stood with his arms outstretched as if waiting to embrace a beloved. On one side of him lay a large lion with an expression of peace and serenity. On his other side, the whitest lamb you can imagine lay looking at me with what seemed to be a broad smile on its face. Behind the man I saw a flutter of wings like a million white birds in constant motion. And they were singing a song I've never heard before, more beautiful than any I've heard.

"And I said to my parents, 'It's over. The race is finally over. You did the best you could. You didn't know. No one knew. Yes, it has been an uphill struggle—mostly with myself and my own demons. You were better to me, I have friends now who have been better to me, the world has been better to me than I've been to myself. I'm coming home now, and there will be no regrets. It's over, it's done. The slate begins anew. I'm coming home.' And the man with auburn hair came to me and said, 'Welcome my son. You have come of great tribulation and have earned a washed robe.' And he wrapped me in a snow-white robe, and I felt young and new, and free of pain."

John again grew silent and shifted restlessly in his chair attempting to reposition away the pain. He made himself comfortable as he could be, and resumed speaking. He seemed trying to say everything that needed saying while he still had time. He turned to face Matt.

"Matthew, I owe you so much." Matt caught a quick breath when John called him by his name for the first time. "If not for you sticking your lawyer nose in my business, I would never have known the love and closeness I feel for all of you here today." He looked at Florence. "And you, pretty lady, you have given me as much love as I have ever known. If I had met you thirty years ago, old gal, I would have taught you what you don't know how." Florence joined him in a soft chuckle and subtly dabbed her eyes with a small handkerchief.

Now it was Robert's time.

"My friend Robert, you have been my friend longer than anyone, and I am grateful. I don't like to ask favors, but I'm asking Florence to let you stay here and take care of her and these other ladies for as long as they need you."

Robert did not respond for fear that he would break down. John's sentiment moved him, but he couldn't believe the ladies of the house would want someone with his background hanging around like a mutt in a kennel with thoroughbreds.

The group sat silent long into the evening. John was too weak to talk anymore, and the others didn't know what to say, how to express their grief. Supper was prepared, but no one seemed hungry. They sat at the table unable to eat. They finally gave up and cleared the table. When they finished that chore, they went their separate ways. Robert helped John to bed. And in the cool, quiet hours of morning when dawn began spreading gray twilight across the island, pain woke him from a restless sleep. He struggled to sit up, but fell back to his pillow. He listened to the vague and distant sounds of three loud, slow breaths, and the early-dawn light filtering into his room faded to black, and the pain in his body was no more.

# Twenty-One

*M*att took care of John's funeral arrangements, except for the dispersing of his ashes in the Gulf.

"I can help with that," Melody told him when he discussed the task with the household. "My godfather over on Bay Street has a twenty-one-foot sailboat that I think will get us to the Gulf Stream and back safely on a settled tide."

"You can sail?" Matt asked incredulously. "You've never mentioned that."

"I don't have to tell you all my secrets," she said, but she was thinking, *I would love to share everything with you.* When Matt did not respond, she said, "My dad and my godfather started teaching me when I was ten."

Matt looked at Melody for a long time. Finally he muttered, "I'm impressed." After a short pause, he said. "You mentioned your father. You've never talked about your parents. What can you tell me about them?"

"My dad is a machinist. The best. Incidentally, he's also the best dad. When the plant in Savannah downsized in 2009, he lost his job. He and Mom moved to Houston to take a job there."

"I'm sorry they had to leave you."

"Yes. I miss my mom and her pecan pie. I bet you would like that—and her. And she would like you. She always liked my boyfriends. She liked to say that I know how to pick them.

Sometimes I thought she liked them better than I did." Melody laughed softly.

On the day John's ashes were returned to Matt, the weather was perfect. The marine forecast for the next three days was for continued calm winds and waters. The next day the group readied the boat and prepared to sail. Florence declared that she was too old to sail. With painful reluctance Robert refused to go because of his fear of the ocean. Hannah had an important exam in school that she could not miss.

"It looks like we're going to be the final undertakers, madam," Matt said to Melody.

"That's all right. We can handle it. You ready to sail?"

"Eye, eye, captain. What do I need to do?"

"Help me launch, then get in the boat. I'll instruct you from there."

"Aye, aye, my captain. I live to serve you."

*How I wish that were true,* Melody thought. "Don't commit to a job you're unprepared for, buster." She knew that Matt caught the yearning in her voice and she didn't care. She had not been with a man since the night on the beach with him. It was time for one of them to make a move and let the chips fall. If Matt did not want her, one of the men she had turned down would.

The boat sailed smoothly out to sea, the shoreline disappearing behind them. The course was set, and the couple sat on the back of the vessel watching miles of water pass beneath them, and drinking in the feel of the cool, misty air and the beauty and freedom of the open sea. They spoke of the glories of life and how death takes it all away.

"I guess we exchange one beauty for another."

"I suppose so," Matt responded. "For the philosopher that was certainly true."

"It's such a shame for some people to waste the life we are given here."

Matt ignored the innuendo of her statement. "I suppose so."

Melody would not let it go. She had a point to make but was unsure of how to approach it. She feared addressing it directly and taking the chance of halting any forward momentum she may have started. She felt her stomach twist into a hard knot and the back of her neck stiffen, but she had to continue the route she had begun. She could not turn back. The bridge behind her was washed away by compelling desire to reach her destination. She slid closer to Matt and looked into the profile of his face.

"That woman you were seeing. Is that still a thing with y'all?"

The question surprised Matt and made him uncomfortable. He did not want to talk about Carolyn. He was afraid to be with her at the present, but she still held a roomy corner in his heart that he feared could not be filled by anyone but her. He had hoped his neglect to speak to her or see her would arouse awakening, and she would be the woman he could share his life with forever. Deep in his heart, he felt strongly that he was foolish for trying to hold on to Carolyn. In college he had read Maugham's autobiographical novel, *Of Human Bondage,* and was aware of obsessive romantic attachment. Lord knows, Professor Steinberg had hammered on it so intently that an indelible crease would remain in his brain forever. Carolyn was the only obsession in his life since he had begun recovering from his addiction to wealth accumulation. He wished he could be done with Carolyn, but when he was away from her he missed the love they had known at Harvard.

"I don't see Carolyn. But I have to be honest with you, I miss her."

"Thank you for your honesty. Do you think things will work out for you?"

"I have doubts—and hopes."

*Why did he have to be so damned honest?* What are you going to do?"

"I don't know. Maybe I should get on highway 80 and keep driving until I get to the West Coast. I've never thought about living in California, but maybe I should. It's beautiful there, I'm told."

"You would leave Tybee?"

Matt thought a moment. "No. I guess not. I don't know what to do."

"Sometimes the answer to our dilemmas is right under our noses. Have you ever thought about that?"

"What do you mean?" Matt knew what she meant, but he had to ask.

Melody would not stop now. She had gone too far to turn back. She looked down and studied the shellacked crème-colored flooring of the boat's deck and thought of the love and care and patience her godfather had put into the seven years of crafting the boat. He finished it the week before she turned ten. She and her dad sailed with him on the boat's first voyage. The moon was full, and they spent the night at sea near Grey's Reef. She remembered listening to the snoring of the men below deck when she could not sleep and stood for hours staring at the unencumbered glade on the water. It was the widest, longest, and most beautiful moon glade she would see again for a long time. She finally slept, but awoke in time to see the breathtaking sun rise out of the water. In the imagination of the romance of her soul, she watched the sun shake off water and smile at her. She felt suspended somewhere between heaven and the sea. She lifted her head and felt her lips break into an expression of rapture and delight. A feeling like awakening on Christmas morning enveloped her in controlled excitement. She feared that if she set the exhilaration inside her free, the men below deck would awaken. This moment was hers. If she shared it, maybe it would disappear never to be recaptured.

She allowed the memory to slip away and her mind to flow back to the present. Turning again to his profile, she said, "Matt, you do know how I feel about you, don't you?"

He did not want to answer. Carolyn was in his heart, but he did not want to risk losing Melody. In a perfect world, he would have them both; in the real world, he would eventually have to choose.

He looked at Melody with the sun shining full on her face. He suddenly found himself looking for flaws, but saw none. The

148

squinting of her blue eyes could not dampen their sparkle. He felt an urgency churning inside, stirring him to reach out and take her in his arms. He knew she would welcome any advances he made. But what about Carolyn? He remembered Melody's admonition earlier that day: Don't commit to a job you are not prepared for.

The feeling was disrupted by a sudden thunderstorm. Heavy rains whipped the boat into a frenzy of motion. A crosswind gusted from the south and the boat twisted sideways, sliding down the crest of suddenly menacing waves. Melody jumped to her feet and frantically began doing things that Matt did not understand. "Help me with the mains'l and grab that stays'l," melody screamed.

"What the hell is a mains'l and a stays'l?" Matt knew he had to do something or they would lose the boat.

"'Main sail,' landlubber, and 'stay sail.' Help me here! We'll study the language later. Grab this rope and hold it."

Matt did as he was told, but despite their struggles the boat rode high on a large wave and slid violently to the bottom of a deep trough. Matt clung to the side of the boat and watched as waves rose within six inches of the top of the vessel's hull. Melody continued feverously working the sails. Fifteen or twenty anxious minutes passed, and the rains ceased and the winds subsided, and peace returned to the sea as if the calmness had never been fractured. A double rainbow appeared against a blue sky. The boat steadied and, relieved, the couple embraced, and the voyage continued without further incident.

# Twenty-Two

The boat continued on its eastern journey, and Melody calculated that they had reached the Gulf Stream.

"I guess we should say some words," Matt said. "I don't know any that would be appropriate, do you? Could we just say the Lord's Prayer?"

"I don't think John would like that. You know he liked to do his own praying. You spread the ashes and I'll do some words." Melody handed Matt the urn. They watched the wind and the ocean take John Marion Wayne unto their own. "Lord, he's in your care, now. We've done all we can for him. He doesn't require much, Lord. Find him a bridge on a heavenly highway and give him the directions to the nearest library and he will be content. Amen."

"Amen," Matt repeated.

They reset the sails and began the return voyage, silent for a long time, feeling the loneliness of a lost friend. The boat glided low on the easy tide. The winds had turned calmer than before, and the boat joined the sailors in silence as if it, too, felt sadness.

The couple marveled at the spaciousness and peace and freedom surrounding them, and thought how wonderful it would be if the whole world could feel the contentment and harmony they felt at the moment. Matt stood and walked around the deck thinking, remembering. Melody remained seated and watched his movements. He removed his shirt, still drenched from the storm. Melody noted that he was not muscular in the sense of being excessively brawny, but he was well built. She had never seen that much of his body in clear light. When he walked the naked muscles of his upper body moved with his every motion unhindered by unnecessary flesh. A stirring began in her mind, spirit, and body, a yearning she often felt in Matt's presence, but now irresistibly powerful.

He disappeared below deck and she missed him. She felt like screaming after him to come back, to be with her and not leave her alone as he had done for more than a year now.

Matt walked to the bottom of the steps and stood looking at her for several minutes. His expression began to mirror her feelings. He felt himself being drawn to her. He needed to go to her, but he resisted the urge. They continued to gaze into each other's eyes. Matt's next awareness was of his footsteps moving slowly toward her.

Melody read his expression and the movement of his body. She stood and felt her feet gliding briskly across the smooth finish of the boat's deck. When she reached Matt, she threw herself into his arms. He lifted her and drew her to him, holding her as if she would fall away and be gone forever. They shared a long, hungry kiss. He moved backward to the steps to the cabin below deck, never letting her go. They fell onto the nearest bunk; and the warming sun, the cooling mist of the ocean, and the planet Earth swirled about them in a hurricane of passion losing them in each other, and they did not care that they were lost. They were where they wanted to be, needed to be, and the rightness of where they were embraced them in ecstasy they had never before known....

When hours later they returned on deck, the shoreline rose above the tide. The wind had calmed even more, and they decided to furl the sails and spend the night on board the boat.

At dawn of the next day, they awakened to low hanging, dark clouds. The trade winds had returned, blowing the boat toward the island. For a time Matt had slipped the bonds of responsibility and reality. But with the docking of the boat, yesterday's life would return. And as is often the case, especially with the male of the species, passions of the night are swept away in the light of day, and second thoughts fill the mind with doubts of what is. It is sometimes then that the mind fills itself with memories of another time and place, with memories of what was, and with memories of what could still be—especially in the thoughts of the male of the species.

# Twenty-Three

The next morning Matt sat in his office thinking of the day before. "I love you," were the last words he had heard from Melody when he gently kissed her goodbye at her duplex door. He had muttered something like "me too," and left her looking after him. *Damn, I may have messed up again.*

A rattling at the door interrupted his thoughts. Someone seemed to be having difficulty opening it. He stood up and walked to the door. Florence sat outside in her wheelchair looking at him. He helped her into the office.

"If I was in my old frame of mind, sonny, I'd be giving you a big cussing right now. When are you going to get that bleeping door fixed? It's no wonder you don't do more business than you do. Who wants a lawyer that can't even fix his bleeping door? Sonny, you've got to get with the program!"

"I'm sorry, Miss Florence. I'm going to get that friggin door fixed this very day. There. I've cursed for you. Does that make you feel better?"

"Tell me something, sonny, what does 'friggin' mean anyway?"

Matt explained that the word was a euphemism and what it represented.

"Oh, my." A hand sprung to her suddenly opened mouth. "Is that what I've been saying all these years?"

"Afraid so."

"Oh, my." Miss Florence shook her head muttering, "uh, uh, uh." In a few seconds, she began dawdling with the purse on her lap and straightening the ruffles in her dress. Matt gave her time to compose herself. When she was ready, he asked, "What can I do for you, Miss Florence?—after I agree to fix the door, I mean."

"Don't get sassy with me, sonny. Just because the philosopher called you by your real name don't mean you can get all uppity on me."

"Yes ma'am. I understand that. I'm sorry." Matt stifled the grin he was feeling.

"I want you to write me a will."

"Oh you don't need a will. You've got plenty of time for that."

"Don't patronize me, sonny. I need a will, and I want you to write it without delay."

Matt noted the urgency in her voice. "Yes ma'am. Tell me what you want to do, and I'll get right on it."

"I will. But first I want to know what something like that will cost me. I've got the money to pay. I've got paying boarders now, you know."

"Yes ma'am. And lovely paying boarders they are."

"You're getting sassy again, sonny. I don't think Robert would approve of you calling him 'lovely.' Just write the bleeping will and tell me what I owe you."

Matt leaned forward over his desk and punched on a voice recorder.

"I want to sell my house to Hannah. We've already talked about it and agreed on a price." Florence opened her purse and took out a small slip of paper and pushed it across the desk. "This is the price we agreed on."

Matt picked up the note and read it. "That's very reasonable. You can get a lot more than that, you know. Hannah has the money now."

"I know that, sonny. I don't need you to tell me that."

"Sorry. Just trying to be the lawyer you insist on paying for."

"Be my lawyer and write the will. Now, listen to me. Write in there that Hannah agrees to let Robert live there and take care of the place for as long as he wants to stay." Florence opened her purse again and withdrew a small slip of paper. She slid it across the desk. "She is to let him keep his room and pay him this salary every week. We've talked and she's OK with it."

Matt picked up the note and looked at it. "This, too, is reasonable, Florence."

"And after my funeral expenses, I want you to give a quarter of my estate to the church and the rest to these five charities." She slid another slip of paper across the desk.

"But what is the urgency to write your will at this particular time?"

Florence didn't answer for a long time. She opened her purse and pulled out a small handkerchief and dabbed at her nose. Tiny streaks of red began to trek across the whites of her eyes. She took a deep breath and began speaking softly.

"I'm not well, Matt. I've been sick a long time. Melody and Hannah have been taking turns getting me to the doctor, my cardiologist. I've sworn them to secrecy. I especially didn't want to burden John with my troubles. He's already had enough to deal with in his lifetime. And I don't want Robert to know. He takes things so hard. He's such a sweet and gentle soul," she added and then grew silent.

Matt turned off the voice recorder and sat quietly waiting. Florence had not said all she wanted to say, and she would continue in her own time. He stroked his chin thoughtfully and waited. When she was ready, Florence spoke again.

"I have four seriously blocked arteries, 'occluded,' the doctors call it. The doctor said my chances of surviving the surgery are about fifty percent. I'm eighty-seven years old, Matt. In spite of everything, I've lived a good life and I don't want to take a chance on going that way. I'm ready to go in a natural state. If I had feared death before John came into my life, I certainly don't now. He taught me how to be unafraid." Florence paused again, thinking on poignant memories of John, seeming to caress them at once and then to purge herself of the sensation of abandonment and desolation.

"The rest of y'all never knew, but John and I often talked together. I grew to love him, and he loved me. When he died, my spirit went with him. I am mightily blessed and should be ashamed for what I'm about to say, but I'm ready to go. I want to be with John and continue those long talks we had." She paused and raised her head. She fumbled with the handkerchief in her hand and gazed out the window, appearing to see something visible to her eyes only. "John had so much to share, and I want to hear it all." Florence again fell silent, and Matt knew that she was finished with what she wanted him to know.

"Miss Florence, I'll have your will ready before the end of the day. I'll bring it by and you can sign it, and the girls can witness it."

"Thank you, Matt. Be sure to bring the bill for your fee. And remember don't let Robert know what we are signing."

"Yes ma'am, I'll keep that in mind."

Matt helped her through the door and stood watching her wheelchair roll out of sight. He immediately went to work on her will. His computer program guided him through the process, and in a short while the document was finished. He placed the will in a manila envelope and stood up to deliver it and collect the fee. He was thinking about a modest price that Florence would believe. He did not want her money, but he would not deprive her of the pride and dignity she would know from the paying. He walked toward the door and the phone rang. He turned back and lifted the receiver.

"How have you been? I haven't heard from you in a while." The voice was familiar, dreaded and welcome in the same stroke. How would he handle the call?

"I've been fine, Carolyn." He paused for a moment and the phone went quiet. To break the silence, he said, "You remember my friend, John? He passed away."

"Well, he was a burden anyway, wasn't he?"

Matt probably expected a response like that, nevertheless the words shocked him. "I've never thought of John as a burden. The people you care for are not burdens. He was a good man and a good friend."

"With all his education, what did he ever accomplish?"

"I've come to know that everything in life is not about accomplishment of the concrete. But just for your information, he contributed a lot to the people who loved him."

"Maybe so, but that's not why I called. I'm going home for the Memorial Holiday. I want you to come with me."

Matt thought for several seconds without speaking. Following the delayed response, he heard, "Are you there?"

"Yes, yes I am." Again he fell into thought. Finally, he spoke. "I was thumbing through my schedule and I have something going that I can't drop at that time." Silence emanated from the other end of the line. Through the wires he could feel Carolyn grow cold. She was not accustomed to rejection and did not like it. The phone came to life again.

"Is the 'something' your little Tybee whore?"

"I have been spending time with a young lady on the island, but I'm sorry, I don't know any whores."

"I have my sources, and I know all about that little leprechaun. I don't know why you would waste your time with a bed-pan jockey. I'm available, and there are others in the area equal to your status."

"She's not a leprechaun. She's petite. And I find her 'status' appealing."

"You sound like the little bitch has you in her clutches."

"I can assure you, she is a perfectly proper young lady." Why was he wasting his time in a conversation that was really nothing more than an indictment of the woman he loved? Did he think 'love?' If he was thinking love, why was he not more aggressive in defending Melody? And then it came to him: it did not matter what Carolyn thought. He did not care. Her opinion mattered not at all.

"Are you in love with her?"

Matt thought for a long time without speaking. Did he feel it? Should he say it? Finally, he said resolutely, "Yes. Yes. I am in love with Nurse Melody Malone. And you, Carolyn, you have a wonderful life." He quickly dropped the phone onto its cradle. He visualized in his mind the anguish on the other end of the line. A satisfied smile claimed a happy place on his lips. He had thought it and felt it. Now he had said it. It was clear now. He was in love with Nurse Melody Malone.

# Twenty-Four

*M*att walked to Florence's house and found her sitting quietly in a rocking chair on her deck. He noticed she was breathing hard.

"Come on up and have a seat, Matt. The girls are finishing dinner. I got a little winded and had to sit a spell. But don't worry, I've taught them well. The meal will turn out fine."

"I didn't come to eat, Miss Florence. I brought the papers you wanted. You'll need to have two witnesses sign them, and I'll have them recorded tomorrow. I have a copy for you and one for Hannah if you want her to have it."

"I do, Matt. I want everything communicated clearly and done proper. Now, about the fee. Don't think for a minute I'm going to forget that."

"I don't know, Miss Florence. I don't do much will drawing. How does seventy-five dollars sound?"

"How would I know? I've never made a will. Step inside the door there and find my purse beside the Bible on that table. Bring it to me."

Matt brought the purse and Florence sat fumbling through its contents. She took out some bills and fidgeted with them a while. She looked at a twenty and thought for several seconds. A ten followed and she repeated the fidgeting and thinking process as she retrieved and replaced several bills slowly. This went on for a minute or two. Amused, Matt sat silently watching her. When she was satisfied that she had fidgeted and thought enough, she folded two twenties and a ten and handed them to the attorney.

"Thank you, sonny. That is good enough." She pointed to the money in Matt's hand. "You lawyers always charge too much. A body would think that bleeping will was printed on platinum paper with gold ink."

"Yes ma'am. Maybe I did fudge a bit. Thank you for catching that error." With a mock-serious expression on his face, Matt placed the money in the pocket of his shirt.

"You aren't fooling me, sonny. If I was still a cussing woman, I'd tell you to go to hell." Matt laughed and Florence's chair began to slowly rock. She laid her head on the back of the chair and looked up at the ceiling. She closed her eyes and began softly humming *You Are My Sunshine*. Matt leaned back in his chair and propped his feet on the porch railing. He closed his eyes and listened to Florence's humming. As he listened, a vision of Melody danced like an elegant ballerina into his mind. *How appropriate the song,* he thought.

Matt dialed a number and spoke into the phone. "Do you know what today is?"

"Of course. It's Cinco de Mayo," Melody answered.

"Well, it is that, but have you noticed how bright the moon over the ocean is lately?"

"I have noticed. It's beautiful."

"For the past several nights, it has been what is called a 'Full Flower Moon.' Tonight it will be full, a spectacular sight, a Super Moon."

"What makes it 'super'?"

"The moon will be at its perigee, closest to Earth this year."

"How close will it be?"

"I heard a local TV meteorologist say it's about two hundred thousand miles."

"Wow! That's close for an object that size."

"Wow is right. I want you to watch it with me on the beach tonight."

"Sure, I can do that." *What is he up to?* She had not seen Matt since their return from scattering John's ashes.

The couple decided on a time and met at the pavilion. Melody arrived before Matt. A few minutes later he appeared and they shared a long embrace. Matt kissed her lightly on the forehead. It was a Saturday night and the pier and pavilion were crowded with tourists. Some smiled and walked on by; others ignored them. Matt took Melody's hand and led her from the pier onto the moist sand still warm from the day in the sun. At the bottom of the pier, they stood looking at the moon that seemed so close they could touch it, or at the very least transport themselves there by helicopter. After a while they began walking along the sand tasting the humidity and breathing the clean pristine air. The tide was at ebb, the sea calm. Despite a brisk breeze from the south, the night had grown sultry. They neared the little palm grove where they had spent their first night together. Matt guided her to the trough between two sand dunes.

*That's the way men are,* Melody thought. *He ignores me for days then gets all horny and calls me with that romantic talk about the moon.* She was angry and disappointed that this appeared to be nothing more than a booty call. Maybe she should have resisted his advances from the git-go. What difference would it have made? Nothing would ever come of their relationship anyway. What was she thinking, giving in to him so easily? As the questions fleeted through her mind, she knew she needed him desperately and would surrender to his advances.

Matt removed his shirt and placed it on the sand and gently sat Melody on it. They leaned back on their elbows and stared at the moon.

Melody wished he would take her in his arms or lie on her lap or do anything that would show her he cared and wanted to be near her. Matt made no move toward her, and they continued looking at the moon and making small talk.

Melody felt an overwhelming need to touch him, to have him touch her, but anger and disappointment would not allow her to move to him.

161

The breeze floated across the water picking up cool moisture undulating across the sand to where they lay. Matt turned his focus from the moon and looked at Melody with the yellow light glowing on her face. She could feel him looking at her. She tried hard and managed to ignore him. He sat up and put an arm around her waist. He reached into his pocket and took out a small case. Melody noted the movement and assumed he was searching for a condom. He held the box in his hand and with a thumb flipped the top open on its hinges. He took out a small, round object and let it slide onto the end of his pinky finger. He leaned his head on her shoulder and pointed at the bright light in the sky above them.

"Look right there," he said pointing. "There's just one tiny little trail of darkness like a shadow or a valley. See it?" He wiggled his pinky finger in the moonlight.

"No, I don't see any dark spot. It's all bright and beautiful." Melody did, indeed, see the tiny shadow. But if he wanted to moon watch, make love to her, then leave her at her doorstep alone, he could watch the damn dark spot by himself.

"Right there. Follow my pinky." He moved his finger near her face and traced a line to the vision in the sky. She inhaled a deep breath and held it. She looked at the object on Matt's finger and at him. Surprise and joy glowed on her face, brighter than the light from the moon. Finally, she started breathing again and looked at Matt.

"Is that what I think it is?" She couldn't believe it. Her joy suddenly vanished. Was the ring for Carolyn? Had he brought her to this sacred place to tell her he was marrying another woman?

"It is what you think it is, my darling, and I want you to wear it. Will you?" Melody took another deep breath and froze. When she could catch her breath, she answered. "Of course I will. Put it on my finger! Put it on!"

In the excitement and eagerness of the moment, the ring dropped onto the soft sand. Melody scrambled to catch it. Disturbance in the sand buried the ring. She and Matt scrambled to their knees slapping at the sand, searching for the lost treasure.

"Wait a minute. Wait a minute." Matt cried. "Let's be calm." The lawyer in him had taken over. "The ring has to be right here in this spot." Matt drew a circle on the ground. "Now, all we have to do is carefully and calmly sift the sand until we find it."

They scooped up sand and watched carefully as it fell through their fingers. This continued for a long time, but the ring was not to be found. Melody began to sob softly. Matt stopped searching and took her in his arms. They lay back on the sand with Melody's head resting on his shoulder.

"It's OK," Matt soothed her. "That little diamond was not deserving of you anyway. I'll buy you another one more appropriate for the love I feel for you." Melody stopped crying and laughed softly.

"Oh, Matt. I do love you so." She sat up and lay across his chest and kissed him. He caressed her body and found her eager for more than the warm feel of his hand, and the night for them ceased to be about a ring or the moon. They lost themselves in an overpowering whirlpool of passion, and nothing else on the moon or on the earth mattered.

# Twenty-Five

*T*he lovers dressed and lay on the beach all night, and when the morning sun peeked over the pier, Melody was the first to wake. She opened one eye and squinted into the sun's reflection on the sand. She moved Matt's arm from hugging her softly in a spooning position. She rolled onto her back and stretched and yawned. Suddenly, she turned on her side facing away from Matt. She remembered something glittering on the sand when she had first opened one eye. Fully awake now, she raised herself on an elbow and stared at the glittering object lying on the sand. She smiled and reached for it. She picked it up and slid it gingerly onto her finger. It was a perfect fit. She raised her arm and looked at the back of her hand. She laid her body across Matt's chest and kissed him.

"Wake up, sleepy-head. Look what I found."

Matt struggled to awake and focus his eyes against the brightness of the sunlight. "I'll be damned," he muttered. "We must have uncovered it during the night. What a stroke of good luck. That does it. I'm going to have to keep you with me the rest of my life. You are definitely my good luck charm."

Melody wrapped her arms around him and held him close. "I think I'm the lucky one, so we'll have to be lucky together."

"I can do that."

"Forever?"

"Yes ma'am. Absolutely forever." Matt gently lifted her chin and kissed her. Voices on the beach interrupted the moment. "We've got to get out of here. We're breaking the law, you know. We're not supposed to sleep on the beach."

"Oh. Did we sleep? I had forgotten that part." Melody laughed and Matt joined her. "You're a lawyer. You can plead us off."

"It doesn't work quite that way. Good lawyers need to follow the rules, too. Come on, woman. We've got to get Florence and the others to church." Matt took Melody's hands in his and lifted her off the sand. She stood and allowed herself to fall against his body. She wrapped her arms tightly around him. He moved her arms from around his waist and took her hand. "Come on, girl. We're attracting attention. You're going to get us thrown in jail before the day is over."

"That's OK. My big, smart lawyer fiance will get us out."

"Sure," Matt answered. "Sure. You keep on believing that and I'll fly you to the moon."

"You've already taken me higher than the moon."

"Good. We'll rappel from there and drop onto the surface by moonrise tonight."

"Now you are the silly one."

"Then that makes two of us."

"Forever?"

"Absolutely. And that's the truth, the whole truth, and nothing but the truth."

No longer able to make the short trip to church, Florence insisted on going anyway. They sat on the rear pew, her place for as long as anyone could remember. As usual, the plugs were pressed securely in her ears. She took a pen and pad from her purse and began planning next Sunday's lunch. Southern fried chicken, of course, would be on the menu, as well as potato salad prepared on Saturday and cooled in the refrigerator overnight. She would not be able to do the meal, but she would be there to supervise Hannah and Melody.

The preacher introduced the sermon and read the chosen scripture. Florence suddenly slumped onto Matt's shoulder and slid onto his lap before he knew what was happening. The sermon ceased and everyone turned toward the "Florence pew." Melody and Hannah rushed to care for her. Melody searched for a pulse and found only a fibrillation. They laid her onto the pew vacated to accommodate her. Fearing a cardiac arrest, Melody began chest compressions while Hannah called 9-1-1. The chest compressions brought about a weak pulse. After a time that seemed much too long to Florence's friends the ambulance arrived. Melody accompanied her to the hospital. Matt and Hannah followed in his car. Robert rode with them, but he was so quiet he was almost non-existent. They reached the hospital a short while after the ambulance arrived. Emergency procedures had already begun on the patient.

Back at the church, the sermon resumed, but everyone's thoughts were on Florence. After the service, the minister and several church goers rushed to the hospital.

At the hospital Florence was given blood thinners and a full examination of her heart. Following two hours of examinations, the doctors reviewed the results and entered Florence's room with a solemn look on their faces. The tall, dark doctor announced that they needed to talk to the patient alone. The short blond cardiologist looked on intently as if to affirm the other's diagnosis.

"Matt stays," Florence responded in a surprisingly strong voice. When Matt and Florence remained alone in the room with the doctors, they recommended surgery for the next morning. They reminded her of the four arteries to her heart that were more than ninety percent blocked. She was told she had a 40-60 chance of surviving the surgery, but without it her death was imminent. Florence stared at the ceiling for a long time. Matt and the doctors exchanged glances. When Florence finally responded, she adamantly refused to undergo the surgery.

"I appreciate and respect your opinions," she told the doctors. "But y'all aren't God. Whether or not you operate, he will call me when he is ready. I'll take your medicine, but I will not agree to surgery." When the doctors left, she turned to Matt. "This is our secret for the time being, sonny. We'll tell the others when the time is right."

"When will the time be right?"

"I'll let you know. Meanwhile, you keep it zipped, and I don't mean your fly. But on second thought, that might, be a good idea, too."

Matt looked at Florence, a little surprised at her remark after the news she had just received. She saw the surprise on his face and laughed. He smiled and left the room to retrieve her other visitors from the waiting area.

In the afternoon, Melody and Robert went home. She had to work the early shift on Monday. Matt and Hannah stayed the night with Florence. In the morning Hannah went to school and Matt checked Florence out of the hospital and drove her home. When they reached Florence's house, Robert came out to help her inside and to bed.

With Florence comfortably tucked in, Matt went to his office. He checked his voice mail and found nothing of importance. After catching up on the electronic and print news, he walked to a file cabinet and took out Florence's folder. He thumbed through the papers and found her will. He laid it on the desk in front of him and slowly read every word, thinking what a noble woman she was and what a loss her passing would be to Tybee and everyone she had touched.

She had told him on the drive home from the hospital how her final rights were to be conducted. The funeral service would be in the church she loved and had attended for so many years. Her burial would be with Carl and Brenda Lynne. After the racial climate changed in the 70s, she had their bodies moved to the white cemetery in her home town. She had no insurance, but she would have the money from the sale of her house. Matt assured her that everything would be taken care of.

Saturday, June16, broke clear and cool with a brisk breeze out of the northeast. The sky was an ocean of blue that seemed to go on forever. The day before, the sky had been dappled with random islands of white against a blue background. But today was perfect for a glorious announcement. Matt and Melody broke the news of their engagement to the family. Florence was eager to know the big day. No definite plans had been made at that time, the couple reported.

"But I want to get married in the Tybee Wedding Chapel. That much I know," Melody announced.

"That's wonderful, darling. Do it soon. I can't wait." Florence seemed as excited as Melody. Matt looked at Florence and understood the double meaning of her statement. For a few seconds, sadness swept over him and he forgot the joy of the moment. He and Florence exchanged glances and each knew what the other was thinking. She gave him a stern look as if to say, Don't you dare say anything to spoil the happiness that child is feeling. Matt turned away and looked down at the floor.

"I'm with you, Miss Florence. I want it soon. How about it, Matt?" Melody took his arm in both of her hands and shook it happily.

"We'll talk about it and decide later." Doubt suddenly began to creep stealthily into Matt's psyche. His parents and two women had let him down, shaken his confidence and rattled his sense of security. He needed some time to get used to the idea before making the big leap. He loved Melody. He knew that. But maybe they should wait a month or two, maybe live together  for a time. Florence's health should hold steady for a while. A Christmas wedding would be nice, or even a June ceremony next year. All brides want a June wedding, don't they?

# Twenty-Six

*M*att left Florence's house feeling uneasy. He walked home on labored legs and fell into an early bed. Late into the night, sleep had not come. Talking about it and wanting marriage was one thing; walking down the aisle was another. He could not survive another broken heart. He finally fell asleep after closing time of the island's bars and restaurants.

He arose early the next morning and steered his car onto I-16. Like a sea anemone, he had neither eyes nor ears. He was aware that he was driving west on the interstate, but he heard nothing and had no thought of where he was going or why. He thought he must have lost his mind. He needed to turn around, or least figure out what his destination was and why he was going there.

Exit signs to small towns along I-16 flew past his Mercedes, and he kept driving. The distance between him and Tybee Island grew with every exit sign flashing briefly in his rear-view mirror. The next awareness of anything other than passing time and landscape was a vision of a large city rising against the distant horizon. He drove on and came to a sign that read "Welcome to historic Macon Georgia, the Cherry Blossom City." He had never been to Macon, but he had seen it on a map and was aware that the city was located in the approximate geographic center of the state, and he remembered that Macon was the home of Otis Redding, Little Richard, and the Allman Brothers. The melodies of *The Dock of the Bay, Jenny Jenny,* and *Ramblin' Man* flitted briefly through his mind.

He guided the car to the side of the highway and sat trying to clear his head and grasp reality. He rubbed his face with both hands and stared unfocused into space. He could think of no reason to be in Macon. He had no business in the city nor knew anyone there. But as he sat thinking and trying to catch up to reality, he remembered a friend from high school who had relocated to Atlanta after graduation from high school. He had never visited the capital city, but had heard it was an exciting, bustling metropolis. Maybe he would contact his friend and see if she was up to hosting a New Yorker on a tour. He recalled that she had married Murray Relyea, a first-year medical school student.

Matt typed a name into his phone. "Sophia Relyea" produced nothing that he could use. He decided to try the name he knew her by in high school. He tried "Sophia Sparano" and found what he was looking for. He punched a number into the phone and she answered, sounding excited when she learned it was Matt.

"Why don't you come to my place. I'll show you around the city and we can catch up on the news from home. No need to get a hotel. I have two extra bedrooms hardly ever used."

"I'm afraid I don't have much news to share. I'm living on Tybee Island now, and even before I relocated, I had lost contact with almost everyone."

"Me, too, and that's a shame. The world is moving so fast and people move around so much, it's a damn shame."

"Maybe so. But anyway, I don't want to impose on you. I think I should get a room."

"I won't hear it. If you have any fears of me, you don't have to. I assure you I am harmless. I'll give you my address. Do you have a GPS?"

"Yes, I do. And I have my phone."

"I'm in North Metro. Here's the address."

Sophia gave him the number and he punched it into his Garmin. He weaved his way through the Atlanta traffic, not all that different from New York City. In an hour and a half, he parked in front of Sophia's large townhouse. She came out to meet him and ushered him inside to a home with totally modern furnishings, but with a definite smell and feel of money. Matt looked her up and down. Maturity had bestowed on her a loveliness that he did not remember. She was taller and slimmer than he remembered, and darker. Evidence of a male occupant was nowhere to be found. Matt felt disappointment that a husband or lover was not present. He was not sure he could trust himself alone with this inviting woman looking so much like Carolyn. He found it difficult to take his eyes off her.

He glanced at a stack of mail addressed to "Dr. Sophia Sparano" lying on a table.

"You're a doctor?"

"Well, not that kind of doctor. I'm just a lowly psychologist. I specialize in sex therapy, and marriage and relations counseling." She paused and looked at Matt with one raised eyebrow, her head tilted to one side. "Do you have problems I can help you with?"

"Not at all," he lied without hesitation.

"Are you still playing baseball?"

"No. I'm just playing a lowly lawyer."

"I'm impressed. What happened to the game? You were so good in high school."

"Always had my heart set on law. Besides, that was about the time players with names ending in Z, S, or vowels began flooding into the game."

"Oh? Italy is not that far from Spain. Do I detect bias against our Hispanic brothers?" Sophia raised one eyebrow and looked at Matt.

"Certainly not. They have brought a new level of excitement to baseball that we can't help but appreciate. The point is I didn't think I could compete with their skill and commitment. Besides, I took advantage of sports for selfish reasons. Athletics got me into Harvard."

"Oh. I'm impressed doubly. Don't be modest. I know you had to have the grades, too."

Matt did not respond other than to shake his head and grin. The tweaking of his ego felt good.

"By the way, the Dodgers are in town for a three-game set with the Braves. They are playing tonight in about two hours. Want to go? I believe you were a Dodgers fan in high school. I seem to recall something about them trying to recruit you. Is that true?"

"Had my heart set on law. But I am up for the game if you are. I've never seen the Braves in person. I've watched a few games on TV. I'm a Braves fan now of course."

"Of course," Sophia echoed, "me, too. I grew up cheering for the Yankees, but when in Rome, you know." They shared a laugh.

Sophia insisted on driving her Cadillac XLR hardtop convertible. And even though the skies were cloudy with a threat of rain, she lowered the top. Matt found himself unable to resist an occasional glance at her long, dark hair blowing in the wind.

In a short while, they parked at the Brookhaven MARTA station. Sophia bought Breeze passes and they boarded a train to the Five Points station. They walked from the train through Underground Atlanta past the kiosks, restaurants, and clubs. A MARTA shuttle took them the rest of the way to Turner Field.

At the ball park, Matt watched Sophia's long legs slip smartly through the turnstiles, and march confidently to the security table where she offered her purse for inspection.

The game was almost sold out and the best seats available were in the Club Section. The viewing position left a lot to be desired. But with help from the Player Roster and TV monitors, they followed the game well enough. With each hit by a Brave or a strikeout by a Dodger, Sophia grabbed Matt's arm and shook it enthusiastically. Sometimes, she clutched his shoulders and squeezed him to her, pressing her breasts against his chest. By the third inning he found himself wishing for more Braves hits and Dodger strikeouts.

But that did not happen. The Dodgers now led with a score of three to one. Nothing remarkable happened again until sixth inning. Chipper Jones strode confidently to the plate and a thunderous roar blasted from the stadium. Number Ten would surely get a hit or maybe even a homerun and set the home team on a course to save the game. But the fans' hopes were dashed when the Braves star third baseman flied out with two outs already in the playbooks, and the Dodgers scored three runs on a homerun with two men on base.

"Maybe we should head on out and beat the traffic," Sophia said following that chain of events. "It's going to be hell getting out of here when forty-five thousand fans leave the stadium."

"It's your town. You know it best."

After a light meal at a cozy little diner on the north side of town, they returned to Sophia's townhouse. Matt announced that it had been a long day and asked to be excused to prepare for bed. Standing close in front of him, Sophia handed him towels. Matt could feel the inviting warmth of her body and smell the gentle fragrance of her perfume. She leaned closer to him and whispered, "Are you sure you don't have issues I can help you with?"

He stared into her dark eyes. He could tell she was aware of acquiescent thoughts swirling through his mind. Looking at her, feeling her body close to his and her breath on his face, every nerve in his body sensed her as a new and improved Carolyn. A stirring moved in his groin. He could reach for her and she would fall into his arms. A short sweep would land them on the bed she had appointed for him, or they could easily fall onto the plush carpet at their feet. Carpet burns on the knees and elbows would heal quickly, and in the healing, sweet memories would linger long after the burns had healed.

Sophia cupped her hands on his beneath the towels. He felt the softness of hands that obviously had never known a gardening tool or the feel of a vacuum cleaner or the handle of a scrub-mop. He tasted the fragrance of her and felt the sexuality exuding from her body, like heat waves undulating from the blacktop of a Savannah street on a clear day in July. Humidity drenched the air as their breath parried in the moist space between their faces. The delicious enticement before him overwhelmed his every sense. Sophia inched closer, their mutual gaze never straying to the right or the left, never dropping coyly, never rising in question or confusion, never communicating the slightest doubt of what they wanted, what they needed at that moment.

Standing in the hallway with heaven in his arms, inches from paradise on the other side of the bedroom door, Matt suddenly became aware that he had stopped breathing. When he felt the involuntary urge to gulp lungs full of oxygen, he kissed Sophia on her forehead and turned and disappeared behind the bedroom door. He dropped to his knees, bent his body forward and buried his head in the towels lying on the floor.

Minutes passed and he straightened to his knees. He froze in that position for a long time staring into the darkness. When his knees began to ache and his hip muscles began burning and begging for relief, he stood and walked to the shower. He let cold water run over his face and body feeling the guilt of what he almost did, what he wanted to do splash onto the floor, listening to it gurgle down the drain and disappear. He remembered what the philosopher had told him about Jimmy Carter's confession to *Playboy* magazine. *I have lusted in my heart many times, but I know God will forgive me.* Matt was sure of God's forgiveness, but the question troubling his mind was, could Melody? An even greater question nagging at him was, could he forgive himself?

With thoughts of Melody lingering heavily and sweetly in his mind, he slowly dried himself. With no clean underwear, he decided to sleep nude. He lay awake for a long time thinking of Melody and wishing she were with him. Soft footsteps falling in the hallway outside his door intruded into his thoughts. The sounds were from bare feet, and he wondered if the rest of Sophia could be unadorned. Warmth and a feeling of agitation sparked uncontrolled frenzy in his groin. He rolled onto his back and pulled the covers to his chin and lay listening. He remembered that he had not bothered to turn the lock on the bedroom door. He heard no sound, but intuitively he knew that a hand rested lightly on the doorknob. What would he do if the door opened?

More than a minute passed, and soft footsteps turned and faded down the hall. Matt turned on his left side spooning a lonely, empty space where he needed Melody to be. He wrapped his arms securely around the unused pillow and pressed it to his chest. He soon fell into a peaceful sleep. Through the night he dreamed dreams, and in the morning he woke up smiling, grateful that Sophia had not encouraged him more aggressively to stray from the man he wanted to be.

He washed his face, combed his hair, and dressed. He followed the smell of brewing coffee in the kitchen where he found Sophia sitting on a barstool sipping orange juice. Without looking directly at him, she turned in Matt's direction.

"Got coffee brewing. Ready for a cup?"

"Sure. Thanks."

Sophia poured coffee and sat the cup in front of him. They sipped their coffee without speaking. They still had not made eye contact. When both had finished a half cup, Sophia turned on the barstool to face Matt. She set her cup on the bar and studied his profile.

"Matt," she began, "I'm sorry I put you in that unwelcome position last night."

"It's all right, you didn't put me in anything. I was in it as deeply as you were. You are a beautiful, sexy woman, and I encouraged you—or at least didn't discourage you. I have to admit, I wanted you. Badly. But there's someone else. I should have told you. Maybe I didn't because I wanted something to happen with us. I'm sorry."

Sophia straightened on the stool and clasped her hands together in a loud slap. OK. I'm sorry, you're sorry. But I'm glad it's a new day! Let's make use of it. I'm going to take you to the Georgia Aquarium and Olympic Park and show you the big, beautiful city of Atlanta. Satchel up, buddy, I'm driving the XLR. It's sunny out, so the top stays down. OK. Let's roll!"

"I'm right behind you with my comb at the ready."

They reached the aquarium at the corner of Baker and Luckie streets, parked, and walked to the aquarium. This time Matt ignored her long, graceful legs negotiating the turnstiles. They attended all the five venues and the Dolphin Tales show then visited Olympic Park. In late afternoon they were back at

Sophia's townhouse. She stood facing Matt. He looked at her and smiled.

"Thanks for an interesting weekend, doctor. It's been fun."

"Thank you for coming. It has been so good seeing someone from home. Maybe I'll visit you and that lucky girl at Tybee, and you—y'all—can show me around Savannah."

"Make it a long stay. There's a lot to see."

Sophia looked into his eyes. She raised her head and kissed him lightly on the lips. "Good bye, Matt."

"Good bye, Sophia."

Matt had not called Melody all weekend, and he was eager to get back to Tybee. He had some important business to take care of at home.

# Twenty-Seven

*M*att drove south to I-285 east around Atlanta and connected with I-75 south of town. He needed to get home as fast as he could. He had made a call as he left Sophia behind, and someone was worrying and waiting for him, someone he needed to see, someone he needed to plan a wedding with.

A little more than an hour later, he merged onto I-16 east. Three hours later he parked in front of the hospital. Melody would be off duty at seven, but he couldn't wait to see her. He rushed into the hospital and found her seated at the nurse's station working a computer. She looked up and flashed Matt a stern look. Without speaking, she returned to the task at hand. Matt walked behind the counter and lifted her to her feet. He hugged her tightly for a long time feeling the warmth and comfort of being near her. They still had not spoken. Melody clung to him and shifted her eyes to look shyly at the other nurses and staff gathered around the station. When she saw their approving smiles she relaxed and allowed her body to sway into Matt's. He took her shoulders in his hands and held her at arm's length.

"I'll wait for you in the parking lot. We can catch dinner and plan a wedding." Matt released her shoulders and walked away with applause echoing at his back. Before he turned the corner out of sight, he looked over his shoulder to see Melody seated again at the computer smiling with an undeniable pink tint on her cheeks. The color on her cheeks was so beautiful he did not regret that he had embarrassed her.

The date was set for the ceremony to be performed in the Tybee Island Wedding Chapel located on a wooded lot on First Street. The time was correlated with a high tide flooding the marsh behind the chapel creating the feel of the ocean. Flowers, photographers, and caterers were arranged. Hannah cried when Melody asked her to be the Maid of Honor, and Robert smiled with pride—and a little embarrassment—that Matt chose him to stand in such an honored place as his best man.

Nurses from the hospital and other friends jockeyed for the opportunity to serve as bridesmaids, placing Melody in the uneasy position of limiting the number. She finally settled on thirteen and apologized to the rest. Since this was not his first wedding, Matt figured he would need only a best man. Melody's parents would drive in from Houston in a rented RV towing his favorite car, a restored 1958 American Motors Metropolitan, and dock at the Tybee RV Park. Her father would give her away.

The big day came and more than a hundred and twenty-five guests filled the chapel seats, while dozens of others stood along the walls. The prelude began followed by the chiming of the hour. After the Lighting of the Candles ceremony, a trio of Melody's nurse friends sang *Wind Beneath My Wings*. Melody's parents presented a duet of *How Beautiful*. The music ended, and Fredrick Malone escorted his wife to her place of honor and rushed to walk his daughter down the aisle.

Melody and her father reached the designated place in front of the chapel. The pastor read from Corinthians 1:13, verses 4-7, and verse 13.

> Love suffers long, and is kind; love envies not; love
> vauntes not itself; love is not puffed up; love does not
> behave itself unseemly, love seeks not her own, love is
> not easily provoked, love thinks no evil;

Love rejoices not in iniquity, but rejoices in truth;
Love bears all things, believes all things, hopes all things,
endures all things.
And now abides faith, hope, and love, but the greatest of
these is love.

The reading ended with a loud Amen from Miss Florence, and the ceremony began. Sniffles were heard throughout the chapel. Dainty hands raised tissues and handkerchiefs to small noses and moist eyes. The sound of the stifled clearing of a gruff throat from here and there made its reluctant way into the hushed and solemn ambiance of the chapel.

Vows said and kisses kissed, Melody's parents closed the ceremony with a singing of the Lord's Prayer. Matt looked at his new wife and whispered, "I didn't know your folks were singers."

"They're Irish. Of course, they sing."

"And they seem to be so religious," Matt whispered again.

"They're Irish. Of course, they're religious." Melody smiled and touched her cheek softly to Matt's shoulder. He kissed her forehead and gave her an exaggerated stern look.

"You need to tell me these things," he whispered.

"I will. From now on I will share everything. I promise." She snuggled her head against Matt's shoulder.

After the reception and more picture taking, a limousine drove the couple to the Savannah/Hilton Head Airport where they boarded a plane to Orlando. Matt had offered to take her anywhere in the world she wanted to go. He was surprised when she chose Disney World for a honeymoon. She had never been. Neither had Matt.

Epcot was a favorite attraction. They did Spaceship Earth, The Seas with Nemo and Friends, and Ellen Degeneres' presentation of Ellen's Energy Adventure. And even though her program was obsolete, centering on the position that oil derives from fossil sources, they agreed that Ellen was entertaining and cute as a pixie princess, and that the program was generally informative.

Melody watched the night-time fireworks and the Main Street Electrical Parade with child-like delight. But at the Atlantic Dance and at the lodge later that night, she was all woman. She was married now and completely legitimate. She gave herself joyfully without restraints or reservations. Matt returned her freedom with new-found passion and tenderness. He had found the love of his life, a love that he knew would surround him with security, trust, and support, and grow with their years together.

# Twenty-Eight

The week at Disney World ended, and the couple's plane touched down at the Savannah/Hilton Head Airport. They were eager and ready to begin their life as newly-weds. Matt's law practice began to pick up a bit and he offered Melody the option of quitting her nursing job at the hospital. She would hear none of it.

October came and the marsh grasses on the flood plain began their seasonal turn from lush green to soft amber. By the first of December, the plain had taken on the appearance of a field of ripe hay after a heavy winter rain. Florence's health continued to deteriorate and she was confined to her wheelchair. Still, she refused medical treatment, except for medications from the Tybee drug store of Atenolol, Plavix, Lipitor and, of course, a daily baby aspirin. She was no longer able to attend Sunday church and prepare the after-service lunches. On Sundays that Melody was off duty at the hospital, she prepared meals for the family. Someone—occasional all of the family—always sat with Florence through the afternoon. On days Melody had duty at the hospital, Hannah prepared lunch, a skill that she had become quite proficient at from watching Florence. Robert, of course, had the primary task of caring for Florence.

It wasn't supposed to be this way. In books and movies when someone dies, it is always cold, raining, and dreary. But Florence's passing came on a particularly sunny, warm, and pleasant day just as the earth entered winter solstice. Her last wish in life was that she could hold on for three more days to Christmas. But just as life had let her down so many times in the distant past, disappointment thrust itself upon her for a final time. Mercifully, she was by then too weak to know or care.

On the day of her memorial service, church pews filled to capacity and standers bunched  in a line along the walls. She had insisted that the service be simple—and it was. Only one song, *Amazing Grace,* was sung and that without music. The congregational recitation of the Lord's Prayer followed. The remainder of the service was a reading of a short biography and eulogies by the pastor and friends.

She was born in South Florida in 1926. Two months ago she celebrated her eighty-seventh birthday. Her career in younger days was that of a store clerk.

At her request, it was revealed that she was the mother of a daughter. At this revelation a low gasp rose softly in the sanctuary. Mourners looked at each other in astonishment. None had ever known her to be associated with gentlemen callers of any description. Now they understood the photographs on the pedestal at the front of the sanctuary of Florence, a beautiful brass-complexioned girl, and a regal-looking African-American man dressed in an army uniform. The photographs, too, were insisted on by Florence.

The eulogies began with most speakers focusing on a celebration of her life with light-hearted recounts of her abundant peculiarities. The pastor offered a long series of stories centered on Florence's use of ear plugs for the past several years that she did not suspect he knew about. Again, some mourners looked at each other with open mouths. The pastor recognized their disbelief and assured them that, indeed, she often deliberately blocked his sermons. Following those stories, the pastor offered a discussion of how she had given him a detailed description of how her funeral was to be conducted.

Matt took the podium and spoke of Florence's warmth and acceptance of a "poor misguided Yankee," and how he had learned so much about love and family through watching hers and how grateful he was for her bringing him and Melody, and the rest of his new family together.

Melody tried to speak, but grief overtook her and all she could manage was a single statement through soft sobs that she could not control. She squeezed out "I loved her," and returned shaking to her seat. Hannah related a story of how much Florence had taught her about the real meaning of love—and cooking. Throughout it all Robert sat on a front pew with the rest of the family quietly wiping away tears.

Early the next morning, Matt and Melody escorted the hearse carrying Florence's body to South Florida where she was buried beside Carl and Brenda Lynne. When the flower van was unloaded, a floral display was arranged in a circle around the three graves. No formal service was planned. Three souls were joined in rest in a quiet, unassuming way as they had lived.

From their car Matt and Melody watched while the grave was being closed. When the task was completed, they walked to the grave-site and stood quietly hand-in-hand over the fresh mound of sand. After a long period of silence, Matt began speaking. He had no plan and no script. The words began to emerge from somewhere inside him.

"We owe you more than you will ever know, dear lady. You are back with your real family now, and they are with you. Lead them and love them the way you loved us and enjoy the eternity with them that is yours."

When he had ceased speaking he took from a pocket a small silver box. He opened it and looked at the two ear plugs inside. Melody saw the contents of the box and smiled at Matt with her eyes filling with tears. She nodded her head in approval.

Matt placed the silver box on the concrete block at the head of the grave and said, "Hang on to these, dear lady. I'm sure heaven has no sermon that you have never heard. And besides, who is going to plan those Sunday meals if you don't?"

The couple drove back to Tybee Island with few words spoken between them. Matt was thinking of the day's events; Melody's thoughts were of the news she had to share with her husband.

They arrived home early the next morning. Matt slid the blinds to the patio door fully open. The full moon cast a soft yellow luminescence throughout the living room and sparkled silvery on the ocean below. They were tired from the trip and the late hour, but decided to enjoy the moon a while before turning in. They sat on the floor looking out on the beauty before them. Matt wrapped his arm around Melody's shoulder as she nestled her head into the fold between his shoulder and chest. Without moving her head, she spoke into the silence.

"Matt, I have something to tell you." She thought she knew how he would take the news, but she could not be sure. Was he ready for what she was about to share with him?

He looked at the somber expression on her face. Furrows of concern creased his forehead. Was there a former lover he would not want to hear about? A secret child somewhere? An abortion? Did she realize now that marriage to him was not what she wanted after all? He studied her face for a long time. His breathing slowed and a feeling of tightness gripped his stomach. Finally, he had to know. If he was going to be abandoned again, he had to know.

"What is it, baby?" His voice came out heavy with fear and resolution.

"There you go! You said the magic word."

"What are you talking about?" He turned to face her and took her shoulders in his hands.

"You spoke the word of the day. You win the prize."

Matt stared at her in the light of the moon radiating on her face, her blue eyes still serious, but sparkling. He relaxed and smiled.

"And could 'baby' be the magic word of the day? Your baby? I mean, our baby?" Melody smiled and nodded vigorously.

He wrapped his arms around her and drew her tenderly to him. They embraced and he kissed her. "Do you know what it is yet" he asked, doubt and fear now replaced by happiness. "Of course you don't. It's too early."

"I hope it's a boy, just like his dad." She patted an index finger gently on his chest.

"No. It's got to be a girl." Matt paused, waiting to hear what her response would be.

Melody looked at him, wondering if she should continue making her case. She decided against it, concluding that arguing with a lawyer would be a futile exercise. And anyway, the baby's gender had already been determined. No amount of wishing or determination could change that. And it really didn't matter. She was going to be a mother and the baby's father was Matt. How could that possibly be improved on in any way?

Matt looked at his new wife. "My time with you, Florence, and the others in our little group here has taught me that family is the most beautiful thing in the world. And little girls must be the most beautiful and the most precious members because they grow up to be mothers like you."

Melody looked at him and smiled, but said nothing. How could she argue with Matt's kind of logic? She leaned her head on his chest. They made love and fell asleep on the floor.

Matt slept only a few hours and woke up early. He sat up and looked around. He listened for sounds that would tell him Melody was safe somewhere in the house, perhaps in the kitchen or the bathroom. He heard nothing. She was gone. He stood and walked quickly to the bedroom and stepped into a pair of worn sweats. He walked onto the deck. The misty air felt cool on his bare chest. He looked up and down the beach. Near the pier Melody walked toward the water's edge. The morning had dawned on one of those not too rare days when winter temperatures rose into the eighties. She was dressed in pink shorts with white polka dots. A matching frock came almost to the bottom of her shorts. He propped on the deck rail and smiled. He watched as she removed the shorts revealing the length of her legs and a flash of the bikini beneath. She laid the shorts on the moist sand and removed the pink top with the polka dots and let it drop to the ground. From where he stood, it seemed to Matt that her bikini halter strained a little harder at its seams. Pregnancy looked good on her already.

She walked to the water's edge and stood looking out to sea. The warm temperatures of early morning had siphoned up dark clouds from the southeast. As she stood on the brink of the surf, the sun broke free over the clouds imprisoning it and cast a bright, warm glow on the beach below. Matt looked at Melody and surveyed the sum of all things before him. A feeling of well-being came upon him in a powerful sense of security. He inhaled a deep breath of fresh, pristine air, and the world around him sparkled new and fresh and clean and promising, and he was the luckiest man on earth.

# Author's Note

*It takes many hands and creative minds to create a novel, but a note of special appreciation goes to Summer Morris of Sumo Design Studio and cover model Nataliia Lutsiuk.*